About the Author

Nikki Sheehan is the youngest daughter of a rocket scientist. After a degree in linguistics, her first job was subtitling *The Simpsons*. This was followed by a career in journalism. Her debut novel *Who Framed Klaris Cliff?* won the North Herts Book Award for 2015. Nikki is a story mentor for Little Green Pig (part of the Ministry of Stories), taking creative writing into schools in Brighton, where she lives with her family and too many pets.

Nikki Sheehan

ROCK THE BOAT

A Rock the Boat Book

First published by Rock the Boat,
an imprint of Oneworld Publications, 2016

ISBN 978-1-78074-924-2
ISBN 978-1-78074-925-9 (ebook)

Typeset by Hewer Text UK Ltd, Edinburgh
Printed and bound in Great Britain by Clays Ltd, St Ives plc

Oneworld Publications
10 Bloomsbury Street
London WC1B 3SR
England

*For everyone who dared to leap
and knew that they would fly*

Chapter One

Friday

Liam Clark started it. In Regent's Park, with the sandwich.

There were four of them, all Populars, with the confidence and the trainers to match, laughing as they smeared swan droppings on to the slice of bread.

Johnny Emin's lunch box was lying where they had thrown it in the grass. He took out his sandwich and bit into it. He chewed and swallowed. Then he stopped, sniffed it (*like an animal*, Liam thought), peeled the slices apart and saw something, dark and mushy like pâté.

'Miss! Miss! Look what the new kid's eating!'

Liam, with his blond fringe flopping, was pointing and laughing.

Miss was looking at him, frowning.

No, Liam was mistaken. She wasn't looking at him. She was looking over his shoulder, towards the lake.

'The new kid's eating swan poo! Actually eating it!'

No one said anything, so Liam repeated, 'Swan poo!'

Then his smile sank.

His mouth stayed open.

His jaw looked as if it were unhinged.

There was a second of quiet, maybe more; everyone held their breath, the wind paused, and then there was a grating scream, a splash and a whoosh of air from behind as an enormous white thing, hissing like a steam train, charged out of the lake.

Its wings were raised into a feathered cape, and its neck and head stuck straight out like the bayonet on a gun.

The teacher was waving her arms and shouting 'Shoo! Shoo!', as if the massive charging bird were a pigeon, but the swan didn't stop. It headed straight for Liam and pinned him down.

Then everything went so slowly that Johnny, half-eaten sandwich at his feet and swan poo still in the crevices of his molars, had time to enjoy its neck flexing and dipping, its sharp beak stabbing and its muscular wings beating the boy into submission.

'Miss!' Liam was screaming now. 'Help, miss! It's going to kill me!'

But miss wasn't helping.

No one was helping.

Then he started sobbing, and, like a whistle had blown, everyone – except for Johnny and Liam – ran at the swan, shouting and waving their arms.

The swan sat back for a moment and shook its wings, dropping one feather like a spent arrow.

Then it climbed off Liam and headed back to the water, squashing Johnny's sandwich with its big ugly feet as it went.

Johnny waited until it had swum off, then he grabbed the feather and ran.

By the time he reached the infants' school, Johnny was panting and a stitch was cutting into his side.

2

He walked through the gate, past the murals of beaming children, and sat in the shade of a dying tree far from the clusters of parents.

He had been coming here for months, and none of them had spoken to him. Not even the really young ones. He was a teenager; they were adults. It was their place, not his, and he knew they wished he wasn't there.

He wished he wasn't there too.

Hearing the door to Blueberry Class rattle, Johnny stood up and joined the crowd.

The teacher looked through the group and directly at him. She had told him on the first day that she didn't like children being picked up by thirteen-year-olds. Not at all.

'Joh-nny!'

A small boy flew out of the door and into his arms, making him stagger backwards.

'Down, Tiger!'

Mojo opened his dark eyes so wide that they were as round as a cat's, bared his tiny teeth

    and

    yooooowwwled!

Johnny wasn't embarrassed.

He knew that most children act like small humans, not big cats. But Mojo was different.

Anyway, he wasn't always a tiger. The last few months he'd been most breeds of dog, a Shetland pony called Pepperoni and an eagle. For one very long, very slow week, he was a giant African snail.

His mum said that it was something to do with being five.

That wasn't true, but Johnny let it go.

'Down!' Johnny cracked an invisible whip and twirled a moustache that only he and his brother could see.

3

Mojo crouched on his hands and knees, roaring and gnashing, until Johnny tossed him a lump of meat, and, for a second, the playground was a circus ring, the frowning teacher was an ugly clown and the Emin brothers were the star attraction.

They went the long way home to avoid the twenty-four-hour shop swarming with caffeine-fizz-filled kids from Johnny's school. This meant going in and out of a housing estate that had big *No Trespassing* signs, and then along the main road, which was so busy that the noise of engines hurt their ears.

But Johnny didn't mind the walk, as long as it wasn't raining. It meant less time caged like lab mice inside the flat.

He held Mojo's hand as the little boy skipped, but in the heat of the June sun their palms began to slip against each other, and Johnny worried that Mojo would pull free and skip right into the traffic, so he gripped him tighter.

Burnham Tower was the third block on Fellows Road, and Mojo started to tug as soon as he could see it, but Johnny didn't him let go until they had reached the reinforced-glass and metal front door. Then he released Mojo and watched as he raced away up into the gloom.

The lift was broken as usual, so Johnny trudged behind, listening to Mojo's footsteps echoing up the concrete stairs, counting each time the sound muffled on the softer flooring of a landing, until, on the eighth, it stopped.

'You lose, slowbus,' Mojo said when he reached their floor.

'Slowcoach,' said Johnny.

'What's a coach?'

'A bus.'

'That's what I said.'

As Johnny reached into his bag for the keys, he felt the feather that the swan had dropped. He still wasn't sure what had happened back there in the park, but it had been good seeing the bully get what he deserved.

Keeping the feather in his hand, he let them both into the tiny flat. His mum had called it an 'apartment' when she told them they would be leaving their little house in Tooting and moving north of the river to Swiss Cottage. It had sounded glamorous. 'Great views, and so central too,' she had said. 'And no gardening for me to worry about.'

But it was a hole.

The stairwells smelt of other people's cooking, the lift never worked and their flat was so small that Johnny could almost hear his mum and brother thinking.

Mojo kicked off his shoes then ran to the kitchen, pulled back the vinyl tablecloth and settled down with his pens to draw on the table.

Actually *on* the table.

'You're going to have to stop doing that,' Johnny said, not for the first time. 'Mum will go mad when she sees.'

Mojo ignored him. His tongue poked from the corner of his mouth and his head bobbed slightly as he drew, like he was having a conversation with the characters that were running around the circle that was the edge of the table.

He had started it that week, drawing in the hours that sagged between the two of them before their mum got home. And now, Johnny realised, there was a whole scene, a bit like the Bayeux Tapestry. But instead of old-fashioned knights on horseback it was made up of Mojo's superheroes.

Johnny watched as he drew. 'Who's that with Catwoman?' he asked.

Mojo didn't look up. 'She's not Catwoman, she's Super Fur Face.'

'And who's helping her?'

'Itchy Red.' Mojo stroked the drawing of the smaller, ginger cat person with dots all around its head. 'He does really good kicks, but he's always scratching his bum because of the fleas.'

Mojo karate-kicked his brother to demonstrate, then scratched his own behind.

'Ow!' Johnny said, though it didn't really hurt. 'And who's this in the hat?'

Mojo put his finger to his mouth and spoke in a whisper. 'It's Mysterious Black. He's the one who knows all about it.' He spread his arms and opened his eyes wide. 'But he'll never, ever tell, so don't bother asking.'

Johnny looked at the clock. It was still ages before his mum got back.

'Mojo, it's great and all that, but . . .'

Mojo looked up, his eyes as big and sad as a bushbaby's.

'Why don't we try and clean it off? And I promise I'll bring back some paper from school tomorrow.'

Mojo wasn't listening. He was staring at the feather that was still in Johnny's hands. 'What's that?'

'This? Oh, it's magic.'

Mojo scowled. 'How's it magic?'

Johnny waved the feather around like a wand, then pointed it at him. 'It protects weedy boys from the evil Populars. Here.'

He placed it on Mojo's palm, then went to the kettle and started to make them both a cup of tea.

'Can it fly?' Mojo asked.

'Well, yes, I suppose. I mean, feathers help the bird –'

Johnny turned back just in time to see Mojo drop the feather out of the eighth-floor window.

'No!'

'But you said it could fly! I just wanted to watch.'

And it could fly.

Well, it could float anyway.

Swing on a breeze that Johnny couldn't feel.

Swooping far away to the next block of flats.

Then back again.

Until a gust sent the feather

spinning

away

towards

the street

below.

As he lost sight of it, Johnny thought about the swan that had given it to him, and he had a funny sensation in his stomach. Like his intestines were fighting.

'I'm going to find it. Wait here!' he said, and he ran out of the flat, down the eight flights of stairs, out of the tower block and into the murk and drizzle and roar of the London street.

The weather had looked fine from the window, but once he was outside the light breeze grew stronger and clouds knitted their way across the sky, blotting out the sun and throwing a shadow over Fellows Road.

Johnny shivered but carried on, trying to ignore his conscience whispering that he shouldn't have left Mojo.

The feather had to be nearby, and it would be stupid to give up so easily.

He would give himself another minute.

Maybe two.

Three at the absolute most.

And then everything changed.

The clouds, which had looked so innocent, bulged and rumbled and then broke, and the wind whipped sideways.

He pulled up the collar of his thin school shirt, but the slanting rain still hit him like sharpened chopsticks. He was quickly soaked through, then the water worked its way inside his clothes and trickled down his back and out through his billowing shirt tails.

Johnny was still scanning the ground for the feather, but the rain was so heavy that he couldn't see without shielding his eyes with his hand.

Streams were beginning to form, snaking along the pavement, carrying off bobbing cigarette butts and dead leaves. When they reached the drains they teetered like logs at the top of a waterfall, then plunged over and away.

Johnny pushed through as the rain came down harder and harder and the streams ran faster. Crisp packets, old cans and then a dead cat floated past and disappeared.

The water was so deep now that it flowed over his shoes and tugged at the bottom of his school trousers. He didn't care that his feet were soaked, but he was beginning to wonder if he might soon be knocked over and swept away too, like the rubbish.

Then the rain slowed to a patter, and he stopped walking and

   just

    stared.

The sun had pushed through the clouds, and rays, like God's fingers, were stroking glittering stripes on to the pavement.

Johnny let out a gasp because, as the water at his feet began to drain, all the grime and litter went with it. Even the chewing gum that had been trodden into the pavement a hundred thousand times, was peeling itself off and flapping in the stream, before sailing away.

And then the rain stopped completely.

Above him a smudgy rainbow arched through the blue, and the pavement shone and sparkled.

Johnny looked along the silent street. There was no traffic. No planes in the sky. Apart from a few shadowy people sheltering in shop doorways, he was alone in the fresh, new world.

When he got home, his mum was standing at the door with a look on her face that Johnny couldn't interpret.

She grabbed him and pulled him close.

'I thought something had happened to you!'

She sobbed into his shoulder, and his wonder dissolved.

'Sorry,' he said. 'I just went out for a moment.'

'A moment? It wasn't a moment, Johnny! I've been back for half an hour, and Mojo said you went out ages before that. What were you thinking of, leaving him all alone like that?' She pushed Johnny back now, holding him at arm's length. 'And why are you all wet?'

He hadn't noticed that his uniform was sticking to him and droplets were splashing on to the floor.

'It was raining.'

She looked out of the window at the bluest early evening sky.

'Raining? Are you sure? Looks dry as a bone out there now.'

Johnny shook the water from his head as a response.

'Must've been a freak shower.' She pulled him close again. The artificial flower smell from the perfume she wore nowadays hit his throat. 'Anyway, you're both safe. That's all that matters. And you won't do it again, will you?'

Johnny looked through the open kitchen doorway to Mojo. He was still at the table but the cloth was back on. His hands were spread above the drawings, as though he could feel them through the fabric.

'No. Course I won't,' Johnny said. 'I'm sorry.'

'Well, you'd better not, because I was just starting to think I can trust you and now –'

'You can trust me. And I've said I'm sorry. So just leave it, will you?'

Her face dropped.

'Please?' he added.

She nodded and walked into her room.

Johnny grabbed a towel from the bathroom, then went to the kitchen. He pulled up a chair and sat close to Mojo. The heat from his small body warmed Johnny up.

'Did you find the feather?' Mojo asked.

'Feather?' He shook his head. 'No. It's gone.'

'I'm sorry.' Mojo put his hand on Johnny's arm.

He shrugged. 'It wasn't important. I saw a rainbow. And a dead cat.'

'Really?'

'Yep.'

'Ugh.' Mojo was twirling a pen between his fingers.

'Hey,' Johnny said. 'If I get you some paper maybe you could draw me a new feather?'

Mojo checked that his mum was still in her room, then he lifted the tablecloth.

His pictures had spread. There were more of the super-heroes from earlier, and some new characters that Johnny didn't recognise.

And at the end, drawn so carefully that you could see every fine line and a few glistening drops of water, was the feather.

'It's here,' he whispered. 'I caught it in my mind and I put it here for you. So now you don't need to go out to look for it again.'

Chapter Two

Saturday

The thing about their new life, in a leafy part of North London, was that there wasn't much to do if you didn't have money. There were parks, but Johnny was too old to go and hang out there without a bunch of mates. And there was a library, but he didn't have a card yet, and anyway he was out of the habit of reading.

He looked through the window on to the Saturday morning street. Being on the eighth floor meant that he was high enough to feel removed, but low enough to be able to see what was going on.

The streets around his block of flats were lined with huge red-brick homes owned by millionaires, who came and went in shiny 4x4s. And though the people who lived in the three 1960s blocks outnumbered the millionaires, the set-up made Johnny feel lonely.

It had been different in his old street. Everyone lived in houses that were the same. He had known most of the neighbours, and all the kids.

'Right,' said his mum, coming into the living room. 'Get yourself dressed. I'm not having you moping around the whole weekend.'

She was wearing her jeans and warm hoodie.

'Where are we going?' Johnny asked.

'First to the craft shop.'

'Is there such a thing as a craft shop?'

His mum's confidence wavered for a second.

'Well, somewhere that sells tissue paper, string and dowelling.'

Johnny sighed. A day of TV was a lot more appealing.

'Aren't you at least going to tell me what we're doing?'

'We're going to make kites and fly them, Johnny. D'you remember we did it once, ages ago, with . . . with your dad?'

Johnny scowled. He remembered. Of course he remembered. His kite had been the best, flown the highest. He had spent so long watching it with his face tipped to the sun that his cheeks had burnt.

But that had been then.

'So unless you want to go out in your PJs, I suggest you hurry up,' his mum was saying.

Johnny seriously didn't care what he looked like when he went out; he had no friends, no one to impress. But he didn't want to be seen in his pyjamas.

'Give me five minutes.'

The shopping centre was crowded. Mainly, or so it felt to Johnny, with kids from his school. He kept his head down and tried to look as if he wasn't with the middle-aged woman with dyed black hair and bouncing five-year-old.

His mum had been right. There was a craft shop, of sorts.

She let them choose the paper – black, white and yellow because Mojo couldn't decide between making a bee and a snowman – and she searched for dowelling and string.

14

Standing at the till, Johnny watched the other teenagers stroll past the window in groups, arms linked, giving them ten, twelve legs a piece.

Teenage centipedes.

'This is going to be so lame,' he said to his mum. 'You do know kite-making isn't an appropriate pastime for a thirteen-year-old, right?'

She put her debit card in the little machine and pressed in the numbers.

'You're probably damaging my development or something,' he added.

'Not just making. Making and flying, Johnny. And please try to get in the mood, for your brother's sake.'

Mojo was clutching all the tissue paper and jigging up and down on the balls of his feet.

'Hey, Moj, isn't this the most exciting day of your life?' Johnny said.

His sarcasm was lost on his brother.

'Yes!' Mojo shouted. 'Yes! Yes! Yes!'

Back at home, their mum tried to remember how to make a kite. The truth was that their dad had made them last time. But Johnny didn't mention that because, despite himself, he was having fun, and even saying the D word could spoil everything.

They had tied their dowelling into cross shapes and were cutting up the paper. Johnny had decided to make a crow: big, black and menacing.

But when he stretched his hand out to pick up the paper, he suddenly changed his mind.

He remembered the day before, and what had happened in the park.

He reached for the white.

Johnny had never really thought about what a swan looked like. It was a bird, a big one, and that had been enough. But now he considered it properly.

A swan had a ridiculously long neck and a chunky body, but it was somehow more graceful than a duck or a goose or the other birds that hung around the park.

Using the cross as a support, Johnny spread the shape of the swan's body and wings on top, then ran a strip of white along the protruding front piece for its neck.

At the end he made a head, white but with a black mask leading from the eyes down the beak. As he only had yellow tissue paper, he darkened it, with one of Mojo's felt tips until it was a deep orange, like the beak that had stabbed at the boy with the floppy blond hair.

Then, to trail behind, he made long thin legs with wide black feet.

Johnny attached the string to the middle, where the two sticks met, and it was done.

He had created a swan. But would it fly?

He helped Mojo to finish his bee while their mum made sandwiches and lemon squash, and then they set out for Primrose Hill.

It was only down the road, but Johnny felt like an idiot holding the kite, so he handed it to his mum, and he walked a few steps behind them, with the carrier bag containing the picnic bumping against his leg.

They arrived barely ten minutes later. Johnny thought, as he scanned the horizon, that being close to Primrose Hill was the only good thing about their new home. From the top they could see the whole of London spread out like the miniature towns he had seen at Legoland.

But they weren't there for the view.

He wet his finger and held it up, like his dad had shown

16

him, and detected a weak wind coming i
reckoned there was just enough to suppor

Johnny dumped the bag and he and M
unravel the string. Then, on a count of th
down the hill, dragging their kites behind th

'Come on, Moj,' Johnny shouted. 'Faster or the, won't fly!'

They sped up, running as hard as they could, and they were nearly at the bottom, but their kites had just bounced along the ground.

Johnny stopped and eyed the other kite flyers with their impressive swooping birds and dancing Chinese dragons.

'Let's try again,' he said.

Mojo was frowning, but he followed Johnny back up the hill.

This time their mum held the kites high to start them off, but no matter how fast he ran, Johnny's kite didn't leave the ground.

He waited for Mojo at the bottom of the hill.

'Come on,' Mojo called to his kite as he ran down. 'Good dog.'

Johnny laughed. 'I thought it was a bee.'

Mojo frowned. 'It was, but it's a dog now, and I prefer dogs anyway.'

They trudged back up to the top together. Their mum was talking to one of the kite flyers.

'Would you mind?' she was asking him. 'I think we might have put on too much glue.'

They showed the man their battered swan and bee.

'No, it's your tow point,' he said. 'You just need to move the string up there, about a third of the way along.'

'Of course,' his mum was saying. 'I remember now.'

Johnny undid the string, which was tricky because he had stuck it down so well, and repositioned it.

...en he turned to Mojo. 'Here, let me do yours.'

Mojo held the paper bee tight to his chest.

'No, he doesn't want to fly. He says it's scary and he wants to be a dog and stay on the ground.'

Johnny looked at his mum and they both laughed.

Mojo sat and watched while Johnny hurtled down with his swan. The man had been right. This time it caught the wind and took off, rising quickly. Johnny was able to climb back up the hill and hold it by the string, while his swan bobbed on the breeze like the swans on the lake.

On the way back home, Johnny held the kite himself.

Mojo insisted on dragging his along behind him like a dog, but he was happy and their mum said that was the most important thing.

At the flat, Johnny attached the swan to their bedroom wall.

'It looks lovely there,' his mum said, smiling at it. 'I was trying to remember earlier, and it's just come to me: St Hugh. Do you know about him?'

Johnny shook his head.

His mum wasn't religious, but she had been brought up as a Catholic, and weird saints were her specialist subject.

'The patron saint of swans,' she said.

'Why swans?' Johnny asked.

'Well, the story is that a swan befriended St Hugh. It would stay next to him while he slept, and wake him up if he was in danger.'

'It protected him?'

'Yes, I suppose so.'

Johnny looked up at his swan.

'Can we go out with the kites again tomorrow?'

Chapter Three

Monday

'Hey, new kid!'

Johnny knew something was different the moment he stepped into the classroom.

For once they weren't laughing at him. Every day for the past few weeks since he joined the school, they had found his existence hysterically funny. Johnny had no idea why. It had never happened in his old school. Not to him anyway.

But that day they wanted to talk.

He turned to face the boy who had been calling him.

'What?'

All the class Populars leant forward to see what was about to happen.

'Jonas and Lola said you, like, set a massive vicious swan on Liam Clark, and it nearly killed him!'

He hadn't expected that.

'No. Course I didn't,' Johnny said.

'You did! Everyone says you made it come out of the water, and it was about the size of a cow, and it looked straight at you, like you were its master or something.'

'Yeah, right.' Johnny couldn't help smirking. If he was going to be master of some creature it wouldn't be a swan.

A wolf or a lion maybe. Something that could finish off the job the swan had started.

'We saw you do it,' said the boy next to him. 'You sort of signalled like this.' He stuck his neck forward and made a weird cooing noise.

The others joined in, and a rasping chorus echoed around the classroom.

'Then it did the same thing back to you.' He cooed again. 'And then it – *BAM!*' He hit his palm with his fist. 'Attacked.'

Johnny looked over at the teacher. She must have heard what was going on, but she was pretending to read the register.

'No, it was like this,' another voice said. 'Look!'

He heard a thump and a groan as the kid who always sat at the back – the big, thickset one, taller than the teacher – was knocked off his seat and pinned to the classroom floor.

'Ow! Get off!'

Though he was larger, the boy didn't defend himself. In fact, he sounded like he was going to cry.

Then the one on top started punching him and crowing like a cockerel, flapping his arms.

The whole class cheered, apart from the teacher, who was now scrolling through her phone.

Johnny watched it happen just like he had watched the original scene. He felt sorry for the boy underneath this time, but mainly he was just glad that they had forgotten about him for a moment.

Also, he couldn't help thinking that the bully's technique was all wrong. The swan hadn't punched. It had stabbed with its beak and beaten with its wings simultaneously, which was far deadlier.

'Ahem.'

The teacher finally cleared her throat and started talking, and everyone sat down.

The boy behind Johnny prodded him. 'Liam had to go to hospital to get a massive tetanus jab in the bum,' he whispered. 'He's going to kill you,' he added happily.

Johnny tried to listen to the teacher, but she was talking about tests he didn't care about, and clubs and teams he wouldn't join – because what was the point?

'I've got a special request from Mr Hargreaves,' she said, 'about the cycling club. Road safety trials are . . .'

Johnny put his hands over his ears and closed his eyes until he heard the muffled sound of the chairs being scraped back, signalling the end of registration.

He stayed where he was while everyone piled out. For once, no one hit him accidentally-on-purpose with their bags. It occurred to Johnny that by angering this Liam kid he might have decreased his chances of being beaten up by anyone else. Which could only be a good thing. At least he would know who his enemy was.

In the end there was only one other person left in the room: the boy who had been pinned down during the swan demonstration. His mud-brown hair lay in clumps on his forehead, still messed up from the attack, and he didn't look very happy.

'Thanks for that, mate.'

'Thanks for what?' Johnny said. 'I didn't tell anyone to sit on you.'

He frowned. 'Maybe, but if you hadn't done your swan whisperer act it wouldn't have happened.'

Johnny shrugged, trying to look more relaxed than he felt. 'You're angry with the wrong person.'

'Well, you didn't try and get them off me, did you?'

21

OF COURSE I DIDN'T! Johnny wanted to shout. *I DON'T WANT TO DIE!*

Instead he smirked, and the boy smirked back. Then they both tried not to blink, until the boy broke his hold and barged past him and out of the classroom.

Johnny walked up the corridor behind him. He watched the looks that everyone gave the large kid. They were probably the same ones he got himself, which didn't make sense. He was normal-looking, he didn't act like a weirdo, he didn't smell (he surreptitiously sniffed his armpits to check) and he didn't go looking for trouble.

But he was New.

And New trumps everything.

As he reached the door of the science lab, Johnny saw a group of kids gathered around a boy crouching on a bench. He had folded his arms into wings and was red-faced from straining.

'*QUACK! QUACK! QUACK!*' the chorus greeted him.

'Hey, Swan Boy,' a tall girl said. 'We were just making you feel at home.'

Didn't they know that swans don't quack? Quacks were for ducks. That was basic knowledge.

Suddenly the crowd jumped back from the table, everyone laughing and waving their hands in front of their noses.

'You were supposed to be laying an egg, not dropping one!' someone yelled.

'Do swans lay eggs?' asked someone else.

'Nah, that's chickens,' came a reply.

Finally a teacher walked in, one of the ancient sort, with singe-frizzled hair and gold-rimmed glasses.

'Get down, boy!' he shouted. Then he sniffed. 'Has someone been mucking around with the gas?'

Everyone took their places. Even the large kid had a partner to work with – a really pretty girl, so Johnny knew that at some point there must have been a seating plan.

Johnny sat at the back, alone.

'Now, let's just recap what we learnt about last time. The ecological niche – that's to say, the role that it plays within the community of the ecosystem . . .'

Johnny tried to listen to the teacher, but nothing seemed to go into his head any more.

Or if it did, it slid straight out and was replaced with random questions.

Like:

Why did that swan attack the boy?

Why do these things happen to me?

Why am I at this stinking school?

Why did we have to move anyway?

Why can't my mum work part-time?

But mostly:

When will things get better?

He heard a quiet *thunk* as a folded piece of paper landed on the desk.

Johnny didn't touch it. It must have come from the Populars. What did they want now? No way was he going to open it.

'If untreated sewage – that's to say, the raw stuff from your toilet – gets into rivers . . .'

Johnny kept his eyes ahead, but none of the boys from his tutor group had turned around.

Then he looked over towards the large kid, and caught him staring back. The kid looked away.

'Stefan!' said the teacher. 'I don't know what's so interesting over there, but I don't think you'll find it much help in your end-of-year test. Do you?'

The boy, Stefan, looked down. But the girl next to Stefan, all long blonde hair and flashing smile, was looking over towards Johnny. Then she pointed down to her desk.

She was telling him to read the note.

Was he hallucinating? Or was the prettiest girl in the class trying to communicate with him?

Johnny slid his hand over the note, then, under the table, he unfolded the piece of paper and read.

> *That swan thing was soooo cool. Meet me at lunchtime and*
> *tell me how you did it?*
> *L xxx*

Johnny looked over and saw the girl wave with the tips of her fingers.

He wasn't stupid. Never in the history of school had the prettiest girl in the class voluntarily spoken to the lowliest. Except for a dare. Or a joke.

He screwed up the note and dropped it on to the floor.

If it hadn't been raining so hard, Johnny would have gone outside to eat at lunchtime. But that day everyone was forced into the bowels of hell known as the school canteen.

Did he imagine it, or did the talking and laughing and crashing of cutlery against plates pause for a moment as he entered the room?

He walked past the crowded tables, trying not to look, but the girl who had sent him the note in Science sort of shone, so he couldn't help noticing her sitting in the middle of a bench of Populars, talking and laughing. But, thankfully, not looking over at him.

24

Johnny went to the furthest table and tried not to look at anyone either. That wasn't too hard. No one else sat near him, not until the other tables were so full that kids were perching on the ends with one bum-cheek hanging off. Then a few were forced into the loser zone with him. Stefan was among them, but he didn't make eye contact with Johnny; he just sat and rhythmically shovelled sausage and chips into his mouth.

Johnny could tell that no one at his table was the type to tamper with his lunch, but he ate as fast as he could anyway, with his arm curved around the clouded-plastic lunch box, just in case.

Once he'd eaten, he had a problem. There were still twenty minutes before the next lesson started. It was raining even harder now, and the only other places to go were the toilets or the library.

The toilets were out as he didn't have a death wish, and the girl who sent him the note didn't look the book-ish sort, so he walked to the library, grabbed something off the *Recommended Reads* stand and sat in the furthest corner.

If he'd known it was a story about a zombie apocalypse, Johnny never would have picked it up. There was enough misery in his life without the undead.

He started reading anyway, but he didn't get past the first page before he realised that he was just staring at the letters on the paper.

He used to love reading, but now words seemed to stay as lifeless shapes separated from each other by spaces, instead of linking to make pictures and scenes and people he could escape to.

Which was a shame, because it was now that he really needed them.

Johnny put the book back on the stand, then trailed around the racks, past the magazines, into the Reference section, and out again near GP – Geography.

He didn't think he knew what he was looking for, but maybe he did, because once he got there a rush of excitement told him that he was in the right place: NH – Natural History.

It covered less than half a shelf: Bats, Big Cats, Domestic Husbandry, Invertebrates, Whales. And there, at the end: *The Wildlife of Our Rivers and Lakes.*

Johnny grabbed the book and quickly thumbed through, glancing around every time he turned a page, as if he were stealing a look at someone's diary, until he came to Chapter Seven, 'The Swan'.

The most common breed of swan in the UK is the mute . . . The mute swan is resident all year round . . . Adult males weigh approximately 9–12 kilos . . . wingspan of 200–240 cm . . . They are fiercely protective of their young and have been known to break a person's arm in defence of their nests.

That was all interesting enough, but it didn't tell him why the swan might have attacked Liam – he had been nowhere near a nest.

It really appeared to have been protecting Johnny, like in his mum's story about St Hugh. But why? He was certainly no saint. And it couldn't have mistaken him for a cygnet. He wasn't small, white and fluffy either. He was tallish, black-haired and hadn't been called cute for years.

'Swan Boy!'

Johnny lowered the book.

Through the grey metal rack he saw a line of grinning faces.

The boy with the floppy blond hair, Liam Clark, was in the centre.

The girl who had sent him the note was right next to him.

'What-ya–doing?' she asked in a sing-song voice.

'Nothing,' he said, which he realised was Stupid Answer of the Year.

'He's got a book!' said the girl, winning the Most Obvious Statement category.

'Get it!' ordered Liam.

A strong arm attached to a tall, muscular body stuck through the shelves and grabbed the book.

Johnny knew that he would never live down the Swan Boy thing if they saw what he had been reading, so he held on tight.

'Just. Get. Off!' he grunted through his teeth.

Then all the books were moving across the shelves towards him, toppling over the edge and crashing on to the floor at his feet with a series of cracks that echoed like thunder.

Johnny's fingers were weakening, but he was determined not to give it up. Not to give himself up.

'Just hand over the book, Swan Boy,' Liam said.

Johnny's fingers slipped a centimetre. Then the books stopped falling, and an octopus of arms and hands was grabbing at him.

He couldn't let them have it. But he couldn't hold on any longer either.

He made a decision and let go. The boy went sprawling into the shelves behind him and the book flew out of his hands. Johnny had to get it, but running round the racks would take too long. He needed to do something drastic. He threw his weight against the shelf unit in

27

front of him and, slowly, it began to move, and then to teeter.

'Hey, this thing's falling!' the girl shouted, stepping back. 'It's going to squash us!'

Then the momentum took hold and the whole unit went crashing down, landing against the shelves behind, and showering the kids underneath with the oversized hardbacks from the top shelves.

Everyone apart from Johnny was crouching, dazed, under a pile of books.

He took his chance, stepping around the fallen units and grabbing *The Wildlife of Our Rivers and Lakes* from the floor. He put it in his bag, then turned to go.

'And where do you think you're off to?'

The head teacher, Mr Price, flanked by the librarian and another woman – who was built like a cage fighter, with silver-striped hair – stood glowering.

'I was just walking past,' Johnny said.

Mr Price raised a bushy ginger eyebrow. 'Well, you can stop walking and start helping me to put this back.'

Together they lifted the shelves while the seven boys and one girl stepped out from the mess of books.

'He wasn't just walking past,' the girl said. 'We were. And he pushed this thing right on top of us.'

'Well, I heard a lot of messing around first,' said the librarian, 'and several voices, so I'm not sure I believe any of you.'

Mr Price addressed them, firing his words like bullets from a machine gun. 'Have. You. Any. Idea. How. Dangerous. A. Stunt. Like. This. Can. Be?'

One of the kids giggled nervously.

'You might think it's funny, but books could have been ruined,' he said. 'Plus someone could have been hurt. And that's quite apart from the time it will take poor Miss Harrison to put everything back in the correct order.'

'It's going to take all afternoon,' said the librarian, red-faced and squinty-eyed with anger.

'There will be consequences for all of you,' said Mr Price. 'Litter-picking every lunchtime for two weeks.'

There were shocked murmurs.

'Actually, let's make it a month,' he added.

'Just give us detention, sir,' said the tall boy who had been playing tug of war with the book. 'I'm not picking up someone else's rubbish.'

'My mind is made up,' Mr Price said. 'You will all report to the caretaker's office for your protective gear and health-and-safety talk at 3:00P.M.'

Johnny shook his head. Doing litter-picking was like being put in the stocks – everyone gathered round to laugh and throw things at you. At this school it was even worse than usual because they made you wear a luminous green uniform; your humiliation could probably be seen from the moon.

It wasn't fair. Technically, perhaps, it was his fault. But not morally. The Populars had started it; all he had done was protect himself from even more ridicule by holding on to the stupid book.

He wished that he hadn't bothered.

The cage-fighter lady put her hand on the head teacher's arm. 'May I have a word, Mr Price? I think this could be an ideal opportunity to put my little idea to the test.'

She took him to one side and spoke quietly. He listened, and looked over at the group with a puzzled expression. Then he seemed to sigh and nodded his head. She beamed, took his hand in both of hers and pumped it energetically.

Mr Price walked back and addressed them all. 'Mrs Cray has just had an, er, excellent idea.' He held them in a steely glare. 'If you agree to join in with the school's new dance project, you will be excused from the litter pick.'

Johnny couldn't believe it. He was at one of the roughest schools in North London and the head teacher wanted them to prance around pretending to be a daffodil or a falling star as a punishment.

'I'm not doing that,' Liam Clark said, brushing his floppy hair out of his eyes. 'No way. I'd rather pick up rubbish. Lola too.'

'Yeah,' said the girl. 'Me too.'

'It's up to you,' said the head teacher. 'Dance or debris. You have until 3:00p.m. to decide. Those of you that choose dance, report to Mrs Cray in the gymnasium after school. Litter pickers, meet at the caretaker's office to begin work.'

Johnny looked out of the window. There were two glowing green blobs clearly visible picking litter in the rain. It was the last thing he wanted, but Johnny already knew what his decision would be.

Stefan checked that the cubicles were all empty, then he peered around the changing-room door out into the corridor. No one was coming, but he whistled anyway to make himself look more casual as he patted down coat pockets and felt around school bags.

Most people knew better than to leave money in the changing room, but there were usually one or two who kept their bus money in their pockets.

Stefan only needed a fiver; it shouldn't be too hard. He'd managed it twice now, since he couldn't get any more money from his dad's restaurant.

As he patted down a grey ski jacket, he heard the sound of change and he moved fast, sliding his hand into the pocket and wrapping it around the coins.

He wanted to check the name so he could pay back whoever it was sometime later. But he didn't, because he knew he'd never be able to. And anyway, why risk getting caught returning money?

£2.40. It was a good start. He still had a few more coats to check, and there were all the bags to go through.

He moved along the row, shaking coats as he went, still whistling, though his heart was beating hard enough to crack a rib.

A noise from behind made him jump.

Liam and Jonas came in looking angry. They were talking about getting someone. The new boy. They said he was asking for it.

'Oh, God, not you!' said Liam, seeing Stefan. He took a swig from a can of energy drink, the sort that wasn't allowed in school. 'Why are you hiding in here, you weirdo?'

Stefan wanted to say: *I'm stealing money for you, Liam.* But he knew that would just bring him more trouble.

'I was on my way out,' he said instead.

'Well, wait a minute, would you?' said Liam, putting his skinny arm around Stefan's broad back. 'I need you to do something.'

Stefan wanted to say no, but he couldn't.

'Just hold this. I need to check my timetable on the board outside. Have a bit if you want.'

Liam passed him the drink, and he and Jonas walked out.

Stefan stood there holding the open can. He didn't like fizzy drinks much; they made him burp.

He stood for a minute. Then another.

Had Liam forgotten about the drink?

He'd been ages and Stefan needed to go. But he couldn't walk out with the can in his hand. And he couldn't throw it away either or Liam was bound to appear and demand it back.

He looked at the can. He was feeling a bit thirsty.

Yes, his mouth was definitely dry. It wasn't good to get dehydrated.

Liam had said he could have some. So why shouldn't he?

He put it to his mouth and took a sip.

'Stefan De Luca!' The PE teacher was blocking the doorway. 'I wouldn't have believed this unless I was seeing it with my own eyes.'

'It's not mine,' Stefan said.

'Don't lie to me! I just saw you drinking it!' she shouted. 'Come with me to the Head's office.'

'But it's not mine! I was just holding it for someone!'

She nodded. 'All right then, if it's not yours, whose is it?'

Stefan looked at her. A large vein running down her forehead was bulging.

He sighed. 'Nobody's. I mean, it's mine.'

At three o'clock, Johnny phoned his mum and told her he had detention and she'd have to pick up Mojo. It was easier than explaining the whole story, and it meant that she couldn't argue. Then he trudged over to the gym.

Mrs Cray stood at the front of the room with her legs slightly apart, like a sergeant major in drag. She was smiling, and her eyes were wide open as if she were seeing something wonderful.

Johnny was looking at the same scene as Mrs Cray and wondered how she could possibly be smiling. There were fifteen of them, ranging from stunted and scrawny to six foot and obese, with just one thing in common: they had all committed a crime against the school and chosen dance humiliation over litter-picking humiliation.

He stood with his back to the cold gym wall and stared down at his bare feet. They were pale, damp and soft, like uncooked pastry.

Mrs Cray cleared her throat. 'My dear fellow performers.'

'Prisoners, more like,' Liam said.

'I've got a special plan for you, and you're going to love it!'

There was some sniggering.

'Now, I'm aware that you're here under duress.'

'No, we was under a ton of books,' a voice called out.

Mrs Cray smiled kindly. She wasn't laughing at them. 'What I mean is, I realise that you have chosen to be here as an alternative to litter-picking. And I'm very pleased to have you. If, however, you feel after this lesson that you would prefer to do your time in the traditional manner, you may leave whenever you like. I will not be offended.' She paused. 'So, let's begin. Over the next two weeks we will be interpreting a traditional Russian folk tale which has been told in hundreds of ways over the years. It's a timeless story that is as relevant today as it was when it was first written.'

They all shuffled a bit; someone snorted; someone else yawned.

Johnny noticed Stefan come in and stand at the end of the line. He wondered what he had done to end up there – not that he was going to ask him.

33

Mrs Cray was still talking. 'Before I introduce it properly, I want to assign a few of the larger roles so that those of you who are chosen can really get to know the parts. You can begin to live them and bring your very own special magic to the story.'

She bent down to adjust her dance tights, which looped under her huge horny feet, and Johnny heard the door thump as it closed softly. He scanned the line to see who had escaped. There were at least two empty spaces: Liam and Lola had gone.

'But, first, let's all have a warm-up and release our inner dancers.'

There was another waft of air and a soft thump as the tall kid, Jonas, not even waiting for her to look away, ran out of the gym.

The teacher gave the rest of them another encouraging smile, then turned and walked to the front. As she set up the CD player, four more kids ran out.

'Right then, my lovelies, come away from that wall, and let's loo-sen up those bodies. And stre-tch!'

To a soundtrack of panpipes, the remaining people bent and reached and curled and crouched and did all sorts of weird stuff pretty badly. Even the athletic-looking ones had trouble with it, while the teacher seemed to be made of steel and rubber.

'Miss, we don't bend like you do,' whined a boy at the back. 'We've got bits that get in the way.'

'Rubbish,' she said. 'You just need to let yourselves go.'

Let yourself go?

The words stuck in Johnny's head.

He really wished that he could. Almost anywhere else would have been better than there.

'And now,' she said, her cheeks not even pink, while the rest of them were red-faced and panting, 'for something completely different.' She pushed a few long strands of silver and black hair behind her large ears. 'I want you to form a circle and sit with your eyes shut. No one is to peep or I'll give you an after-school detention.'

Someone said, 'You can't do that, miss.'

But they reluctantly formed a shape a bit like a squashed trapezium and, on command, Johnny shut his eyes.

There was silence.

Then more silence.

Then he heard people moving around, and the door swung a few times.

But he didn't look.

After a minute, perhaps more, Mrs Cray spoke in a low, calm voice.

'There's something or someone you love more than life itself.'

What?

No way.

No.

Johnny felt anger rising through his body.

What sort of dance lesson was this?

Why was she talking like that?

He should go. Walk out like the others.

Why not?

He didn't need to listen to this rubbish.

Then Mrs Cray spoke again. 'I don't want you to say anything out loud, but I want you to think of him or her or it, to get them in your mind's eye and hold them there and be there with them.'

Mind's eye?

She was a mad old hippy.

There was no way he was going to do something stupid like that.

No way.

He would just keep his eyes shut and think of nothing.

Nothing.

Nothing at all.

See? Emptiness. Nothing.

She couldn't make him do it if he didn't want –

There was a picture.

It was the old days. His house. Johnny and Mojo watching TV on the sofa, Mum in the kitchen cooking shepherd's pie, Dad in his chair with the remote in one hand and a beer in the other.

But it wasn't just a picture because he could feel it too. Feel the warmth and ordinariness of it.

48 Timbuktu Road, the home he'd lived in since he was born.

Where his height was marked on the kitchen door frame.

Where the cracks in his bedroom ceiling were the shape of the Matterhorn.

Where his dad was going to build a tree house in the tiny garden.

Where everything was OK.

Then the music started. It was classical, which Johnny usually hated, but this was gentle and sad, with violins and oboes, and it pulled him further in, until he could almost believe that he was his old self again.

His mum and dad were cuddling up on the sofa. They were laughing about a talent show on TV. His dad was saying that he could do better, then he started singing along.

Johnny smiled.

'And now . . .'

But, wait – that wasn't his dad talking.

It was the lunatic dance teacher.

Smashing his dream.

'Slowly, gradually, open your eyes and start to come back to the present.'

But he was already back.

The moment she had spoken, the past had melted away.

As fast as it had the day his dad died.

There were just two of them left in the room. Johnny and Stefan.

'That was wonderful,' said Mrs Cray, grasping her hands together under her chin. 'Congratulations on a fabulous audition.'

She looked them both in the eyes, pausing a beat too long on Johnny.

He felt like she could see what was inside.

'Boys, you are going to be my principal dancers.'

She put one hand on Stefan's shoulders. 'You are the sorcerer Von Rothbart.' She moved over to Johnny. 'And you are our hero, Prince Siegfried.'

The other boy shrugged off her hand, stood up and faced her, scowling. 'But we didn't audition. We didn't even dance.'

Mrs Cray smiled. 'You didn't need to dance. Dancing is mere representation. You did something better – you became.'

Johnny was too angry to speak. How dare she do that to them? He felt like she had fooled him.

She produced two letters from a big flowery shopping bag. 'Please give these to your parents. I need permission slips back by Tuesday if possible.'

She was having a laugh. There was no way Johnny was going to take part in a dance of some old Russian folk story. He would have to do the litter pick after all.

In the changing room, while Johnny took off his PE kit, Stefan screwed up his permission letter, and chucked it in the bin.

'I'm not doing no stupid dance,' he muttered.

'Me neither,' Johnny said. 'She tricked us. I'd rather pick up rubbish for a year.'

Stefan turned round and glared at him.

'I wasn't talking to you,' he said. 'So you don't talk to me. Geddit?'

Johnny glared back, then started getting dressed.

The changing-room door swung open. Lola and Jonas framed the doorway, while Liam Clark walked in, filming on his phone. 'Oh, look. How sweet! Fat Boy and Swan Boy half naked together.'

'We're getting changed – of course we're half naked,' Johnny replied.

'Shut it, Swan Boy,' said Liam. 'I'm not talking to you.' He stopped filming and walked over to Stefan. 'Tomorrow, yeah?'

Johnny could see the Adam's apple in Stefan's throat bob as he swallowed.

'Yeah. I'll try,' he said.

'Well, you'd better,' said Liam, sweeping out, taking Lola and Jonas with him.

'What was that about?' Johnny asked.

Stefan frowned. 'None of your business.'

Johnny held his hands up in a *don't shoot* position. He was only being friendly. He shouldn't have bothered.

He finished getting changed and left without speaking to Stefan again.

As he walked home, he wondered why Stefan would have anything to do with Liam. Johnny had known kids like Liam in his old school; maybe, he thought, towards the end, when he had started getting into trouble, he was even one of them.

But that was then. Now Liam was precisely the sort of person Johnny would do anything to avoid.

Chapter Four

As soon as he stepped into the foyer at Burnham Tower, Johnny noticed that something was different.

For the first time ever the lift wasn't wearing its *DANGER – OUT OF ORDER* sign.

He looked towards the stairs as they faded into blackness.

He hated those stairs. He wasn't as fit as he used to be and the first few flights were OK, but by the third or fourth his legs felt tired, and by the sixth he was breathing hard. By the time he reached the eighth he was sweating like a pig.

Johnny scanned the floor to see if the sign had just fallen off.

It hadn't.

He still hesitated for a moment, then he pushed the button and the doors swept open.

Inside the lift was a huge white swan.

It looked up, turning its head to one side as if considering him.

He knew he should have shut the door quickly and phoned the RSPCA. Or at least shouted, 'There's a

*&$@-ing swan in the lift!' Especially after reading about the arm–breaking thing.

That's what the old Johnny would have done.

But he didn't, because everything was different now, and what did he have to lose?

He took a step forward.

The swan ruffled its feathers, but Johnny thought it looked sort of friendly. For a swan.

He took another step.

The swan moved its head again, slowly, considering him through the other eye.

'Is it you?' Johnny whispered, feeling that it had to be the same swan, the one that had attacked Liam Clark.

The swan shuffled its feet, then sat down.

Johnny took it as an invitation and he stepped inside.

The lift doors immediately closed and he was hit by the rich dark smell that he remembered from Regent's Park.

It made him think of

conkers

and stock cubes

and life.

Johnny hardly dared to breathe. The swan took up most of the space in the hot little metal box, and he didn't want to touch it, so he pushed his back hard against the wall.

Meanwhile the swan held his gaze, showing no fear or aggression, and Johnny became more convinced that it was the same swan, the one who had attacked his enemy.

Then the old electric motor began to whirr, the lights dimmed then flickered, and the lift jolted upwards.

Johnny didn't want to keep staring into those small black eyes, so he stared at the panel instead, watching the numbers slowly go from 1 to 2 to 3, and wondering where the swan was going.

Was it someone's pet? It didn't look like a pet.

Was there a swan sanctuary on the fifth floor? Johnny wasn't sure the council would allow that.

Was it going to his flat?

He sneaked a peek at the swan. It was standing now and it shifted its weight between its huge feet, then twisted and curled its neck round and delicately held out one of its wings to preen the perfect rows of white feathers.

Johnny looked up at the digital panel again: floor six.

The swan glanced back at him in between cleaning different sections. Johnny was pretty sure that the grooming meant that it was relaxed. It did with cats anyway.

He felt more confident now.

'You're not going to hurt me, are you?' he breathed, moving his back slightly away from the wall.

The swan carried on preening, and Johnny felt stupid. Swans don't talk.

But they don't usually take lifts either.

There was a metallic *ding*. Level eight. Johnny's floor.

The doors slid open.

The swan stayed where it was, but it looked at him.

Did it expect him to just go home? To leave it there?

No, he wanted to see where the swan was going.

The doors shut again and the lift continued. The swan gave no indication if it was pleased that Johnny had stayed or not. But Johnny didn't mind. He relaxed a bit more and let himself edge towards the swan, breathing in its smell – salty, warm and alive.

Then, too soon, the lift jerked to a halt at the top floor, level eighteen.

The doors slid open, not on to a dark corridor like level eight, but on to the sky. More big, terrifying, open nothingness than Johnny had ever seen before.

The swan took one last look at him, then stepped out of the lift, waddled, and then ran for a few steps, unfurled its heavy, powerful wings and flew off into the grey.

'Wait!' Johnny shouted. 'You can't just appear and disappear like that! Come back!'

Johnny moved as if he were going to follow it – to run to the edge and take off too – but then he fell back. He tried again, but he couldn't get out of the lift.

'Go on, legs!' he shouted. But he knew it wasn't really the fault of his legs.

It was his brain.

He was scared of heights.

It had been going on for ages. When he was ten they went to the Eiffel Tower. That was the first time.

It had been his mum's dream to visit Paris, and his dad had sprung it on her as a birthday surprise. Mum had said the tower was a rip-off, so she and Mojo had an ice cream down below, while he and his dad climbed up the first two flights, then took the lift all the way to the viewing platform. It was nearly 150 metres up, but the whole thing was caged in, right over his head. He couldn't have fallen.

Johnny joined everyone else oohing and aahing at the view, but, looking down over the tiny streets and buildings, it had suddenly felt wrong.

Everything looked small and accidental somehow, like someone could just kick it all out of the way. He didn't like the city looking so temporary. He wanted everything around him to be solid and permanent.

Johnny's dad must have noticed something wasn't right, because he took hold of his hand. Then, gripping him tight, Johnny looked down again, and this time he knew that he wouldn't fall.

It was the best feeling ever.

But that was then.

Ancient history.

And now his dad wasn't there to help him with the doors that were straining and whirring and trying to close on him.

Johnny gripped the cold metal frame of the lift. He wasn't ready to go downstairs just yet. He'd had enough of the flat's tiny rooms that seemed to get smaller every day. He was enjoying the taste of the freshly blown air, the wind buffeting his body and just how much sky there was. He hadn't known it could go on so far.

But the lift doors seemed to be getting more insistent. He looked down at his feet, cursing them for holding him back, and then he noticed a white feather, a bit like the one Mojo had dropped out of the window. It was being blown away from the doorway. He had to be quick if he wanted it.

And he did.

So he moved without thinking, just a couple of small steps forward on to the roof, enough so that he could bend and pick it up.

The doors squeezed shut behind him.

Johnny ran back and jammed his thumb against the button, but the lift made a whirring noise and then, through the glass panel, he saw it drop out of sight.

He held his thumb on the button and waited for it to return, but the illuminated read-out had gone blank.

He pressed his ear against the door. Silence.

'Come on, open up!' Johnny shouted at it, then hammered with his other hand until it hurt.

Kicking it and swearing didn't seem to help either, so Johnny stood with his back pressed against the doors until his legs suddenly felt too weak to support him any more, and he sunk to the ground.

He felt less wobbly sitting on the gritty surface of the roof. But he was worried about how he was going to get back downstairs. No one would be able to hear him calling for help from up here.

His only hope was to get to the edge and attract someone's attention. But there was no way his legs would take him over there.

He was exhausted. It had been a terrible day, and now this?

He lay on his back and looked up. The sky above him was empty, grey with a few wispy clouds, but not the interesting sort that looked like cupcakes or melting dragons.

After a while, despite his fear, he began to get bored. Maybe that was the reason he started rolling. He hadn't done anything like that since he was a kid, and then it was down soft grassy banks. Up here the rough coating of the rooftop sanded his forehead and grated his shoulders as he went round. But after just ten 360-degree rolls, Johnny was at the very edge.

He peered through the railings and down on to the miniature city. He felt sick. So he shut his eyes and counted to twenty, then he tried again. And it was better.

Johnny started to make out the places he saw every day: the supermarket, the park where he went with his brother. And, just past the bridge, his latest school, St George's Academy for Losers.

Then he looked further, the way the swan had flown, and he could see some landmarks he recognised: the BT Tower, the Gherkin; he even thought he spotted someone puking on the London Eye. And there was the River Thames, slicing the city in half, separating him from his old life, where he had lived in a nice house, with a mum and dad, and gone to a school that he liked and had friends who had known him for ever.

Just out of his line of vision, something red pulled him back to the moment. It was his mum dragging Mojo behind her in the street below. She didn't look happy.

He had to get home.

Without thinking, he stood up, sprinted for the lift and hammered on the button. The doors opened and he fell inside.

Johnny got home first. A minute later his Mum and Mojo came in and sat at the table facing each other. Her lips were drawn inwards. Mojo's face was pale and streaked with mud. He had been crying so much that his breath was catching in his throat and his body was shuddering.

'What's happened?' said Johnny.

His mum raised an eyebrow. 'After-school club didn't go so well.'

Johnny felt the accusation in her voice. 'It wasn't my fault,' he said.

His mum sighed. 'Well, it was, Johnny. He only had to go because you weren't there to pick him up.' She shook her head. 'Detention! I'm so disappointed. You promised me you'd stay out of trouble here. What on earth did you do this time?'

'Nothing,' he said. 'I was just standing near some other kids in the library and something got knocked over so we all got detention. Only it wasn't really detention in the end. It was dance.'

'Dance? Don't make it worse by lying.'

'I'm not lying.'

She sighed, then reached out to him. 'Come here.'

He stayed where he was.

'Look, Johnny, I know it's hard for you. But I don't want you falling into the wrong crowd and sliding backwards again.'

Johnny felt his lip curl slightly.

She knew literally nothing.

He wasn't sliding anywhere.

And he wasn't in with any sort of crowd.

She rubbed her eyes. 'I know the move has unsettled you. And maybe we should've stayed where we were. But we were sinking financially. You know I accepted the job up here because I couldn't see another way, not without your dad's wages. And when I heard that his life insurance wasn't going to pay out . . .'

Johnny glanced over at Mojo. His face was odd. Sort of blank. He shouldn't have to hear stuff like that.

But he couldn't let it go.

'There's always a way, Mum.'

'Well, this time there wasn't, Johnny. Not one that I could think of.' Her voice softened. 'I relied on your dad. I suppose he relied on me too in a way. And to suddenly not have him there to discuss it with . . . Well, maybe you're right, maybe I made the wrong choice, but there's no going back now.'

Johnny scowled. 'You did have someone to discuss it with, Mum. You had me.'

She leant towards him and cupped his face in her hand. 'I know that, Johnny. But you're still a boy.'

'I'm thirteen. Not really a boy. And when something affects me I want to be part of the decision.'

'OK, I'm sorry,' she said. 'Next time I will consider your wishes. You know I wasn't thinking straight after your dad died. I'm still not sure I am now. But what's done is done, Johnny. So we'd better just get on with it.'

She wiped a tear from her eyes and tried to smile.

'So, how about you tell me something nice. Anything good happen at school today?'

Johnny smiled back at her. 'I wasn't lying about the dance, Mum. Look.'

He took out Mrs Cray's letter and handed it to her.

She started reading. Then she looked up, beaming, her eyes glinting with the tears that were pooling.

'Oh, Johnny, how wonderful to be chosen for a part like this. I never knew you could dance! You must get it from me.'

Johnny laughed. 'I can't. And I don't want to disappoint you, but I didn't know I was auditioning, and I wasn't really chosen. All the others ran away. There was only me and this other kid left, so she gave us both the main parts.'

'But, Johnny, it's the Prince! Oh, you have to do it.' She was shaking her head, but smiling too.

'Well, I was going to, but I dunno.'

She frowned. 'What d'you mean, you don't know? You'd love it, Johnny.'

'Yeah, but it's not exactly . . . You remember when you told me I had to try and fit in at the new school. Make friends, all that stuff?'

'Yes. And?'

'And, Mum, it's dance! Boys don't do dance.'

'That's not true. Of course they do.'

'Well, maybe some of them do. But I'm not that kind of boy, and I don't know if it's really going to help. That's all I'm saying.'

Her shoulders slumped and she looked away from him. 'It's all right, I understand. You don't want to do it. It's probably for the best. I mean, it's not exactly the sort of thing your dad would've approved of.' She laughed. 'He was definitely into the more "manly" pursuits. In fact, he'd turn in his grave if he knew.'

'Manly?'

'Yes, you know, boxing, karate, snooker even. Your father had a lot of good qualities, but he was a bit of a dinosaur, even if I say so myself. He liked men and women to keep to their traditional roles. So he wouldn't have liked you to do something like that.' She sighed. 'But he's not here to stop you now, is he?'

Johnny felt the anger that he lived with surge.

No, his dad wasn't there.

He had drunk and smoked twenty a day, and never exercised, even though Mum nagged him about it all the time.

Basically, he had abandoned them.

Johnny tried to smile. He put his arms around his mum. 'Actually, I think you're right. I should do it.'

She hugged him hard. 'You'll make me so proud. I know ballet isn't really your type of thing, but –'

He pulled away. 'What did you say? Ballet? The teacher said it was some old folk tale.'

She nodded. 'Well, *Swan Lake* is a folk tale, told through ballet.'

No.

No. No. No. No. No.

'*Swan Lake?* Are you sure it's *Swan Lake?*' He felt a chill run down his neck. 'Let me see that letter.'

Johnny read it, then put his head in his hands.

'I can't believe it,' he said. 'I'm never going to live down the swan thing now.'

50

'Swan thing?'

'And it'll just be me and a load of girls.'

His mum looked a bit shifty. 'Well, not necessarily. The letter says you're doing selected scenes inspired by the Matthew Bourne version.'

'What's that?'

'Well, I only know about it because there's a poster for the West End show on the Tube.'

'And?'

'It's a version for men.'

'Just for men?'

'Well, all the swans are men anyway.'

Swans that are men?

That couldn't be right.

Swans were girly, fluffy things.

Johnny remembered the swan pinning down Liam Clark: the strength of its neck and the aggression in its attack. And the swan in the lift too: the power in its wings as it took off and flew away, and how envious he had felt of its force and freedom.

Swans weren't girly. Swans were masculine.

Yes, he would do it. Of course he would do it.

He had nothing to lose.

Chapter Five

Tuesday

Liam heard the door slam as his dad left the house. He stretched and felt the pull in his shoulders, and he remembered the swan.

'Stupid thing,' he muttered. He didn't understand why it would have done that.

Not to him.

He got out of bed slowly, like an old man, and walked through the flat. The curtains were still drawn. He didn't bother to open them, just made his way to the kitchen cupboard in the gloom and poured some cereal into the last clean bowl.

His dad had left the milk out. There was only a dribble left, not even enough for a cup of tea.

He filled a glass with water and sat in front of the television while he ate the cereal dry, throwing it into his mouth piece by piece.

Liam liked morning TV. It was a bit lame, but he knew who all the presenters were, and he found seeing the same faces making the same expressions every day comforting somehow.

'The time is now 8:15,' the man in the studio told him.

'Time to go then,' he responded, leaving his bowl on the crowded coffee table in front of him.

On the way out Liam checked the cracked mug on the side. There was less than a pound left. He put the coins in his pocket, but it wouldn't be enough for lunch. He hoped Stefan had that fiver for him.

Jonas and Lola were waiting on the corner. They smiled as he came up, like a pair of eager puppies.

Some people.

'Today's the day that swan kid gets a pasting then,' said Jonas, grinning so wide his gums showed.

'Yeah, after what he's done to you, Liam – first the swan and now the library thing – he deserves it,' said Lola.

She gave him a kiss but he didn't kiss her back.

There was someone else he wanted to ask out, and, if she said yes, he would have to finish with Lola. Not yet though. He wanted to get that Johnny kid sorted first, and Lola would be useful.

He took an energy drink from a four-pack in his bag and opened it, though drinking them so early in the morning made him feel dizzy and sick.

'Thing is,' she continued, 'he's new, so it's up to us to show him where the boundary is. Like, how you don't mess with us, cos otherwise . . .' She left it hanging so the other two could consider what might happen.

Liam took a swig from the can, then he scratched his chest through his jumper.

'Don't you think?' Lola was waiting for a response.

Liam was tired. He didn't want to think anything. But Lola was right – a line had been crossed and it was up to him to do something about it.

Besides, it would give him something to look forward to.

He drained the can, threw it to the ground and crushed it under his trainer.

'Yep, today's the day,' he said, and they set off for school.

A group of Year Nine boys were huddling around the school gates for safety. They were the sort of kids Johnny would have ignored before: Leftovers, with proper school shoes and unfashionable hair.

'Hey, Swan Boy,' one of them called out. 'Liam Clark's gonna smash your face in today.'

He said it like it was the best news ever.

Johnny continued walking.

'Let's follow him!' one of them said.

'What, so you can help me?' Johnny asked.

They all laughed.

'So, what are you gonna do?' someone asked.

Johnny shrugged. 'Get beaten up, I s'pose.'

They all looked disappointed. But they followed him into school and up to his form room. All the way they discussed when and where it would happen.

'Definitely lunchtime,' one boy said.

'No, they'll get him in the bogs before that. More private.'

'Hey, Swan Boy, what time do you usually go for a slash?'

'You selling tickets or something?' Johnny asked.

The boy shrugged. 'No, I just don't want to miss it.'

Johnny walked into his classroom and shut the door on them.

'Aye, aye, I smell swan roast!'

'Nah, swan spag bol. Clark's gonna mince him up!'

'Swan sausages!'

'Swan sausages? That's stupid. You can't make sausages from swans.'

The only person not joining in the joke was Stefan. He was probably just enjoying the rest while someone else was picked on.

Johnny sat in his place while his teacher did the register then read out some notices.

'Anyone who is taking part in the *Swan Lake* show –'

The class roared with laughter.

'What?' said the teacher. 'There's nothing funny about ballet.' She continued over the noise, 'Anyone taking part, please go to the gym at one o'clock.'

Johnny pushed back his chair and walked out before the teacher had finished. He didn't care if he got into trouble. He had to get ahead of the crowds to avoid Liam.

He ran down the empty corridors, up a flight of echoing stairs and made it safely to History.

Liam wasn't in that class, but Johnny heard other people making comments about him when they came in. It seemed like everyone knew about the swan, and about Liam wanting to kill him too.

'Something . . . something . . . something . . . imperialism,' the teacher was saying. 'Something . . . something . . . Ottoman . . . something . . . something . . . governance . . .'

Johnny had no idea what half of the words meant. And even less interest in finding out.

'Something . . . something . . .'

BELL!

'No!' Johnny said under his breath. For once a lesson had gone too fast. He shoved his books into his bag and left.

Although he had got out quickly, it wasn't quick enough. The corridors were half full. He stared down at his shoes, but it was as if there were a flashing sign that said *Victim* positioned just above his head.

'Is that the kid?'

'Yeah!'

'Oi, Swan Boy!'

'Weirdo.'

'*Quackkk! Quackkk!*'

'Ha! Ha!'

'Liam Clark's looking for you!'

'Hey, kid, you're dead!'

He needed the toilet, but that was far too dangerous, so he ran to his next lesson, PSHE, Personal and Social Health Education.

The teacher, one of the young keen ones in jeans, stood at the board. In big letters he wrote one word: *METAMORPHOSIS.*

Johnny took his seat and got his book out.

'Books away for the moment,' the teacher said. 'First we will be thinking and talking.'

Johnny groaned. He hated lessons where he might have to join in.

'Right, class, can anyone tell me what this word means?'

'It's a club down town, sir,' someone shouted.

The teacher smiled. 'You're right, Aiden. But what does it mean?'

A small boy at the front put up his hand. 'And it's the name of a book where someone turns into an insect. It means change.'

The teacher grinned. 'Correct. The change or transform-ation of a person or thing into something completely different. In the book that Dominic mentions, a man changes into a cockroach.'

'Ew!' someone squealed.

'But this isn't the only story like that. The classics, Ancient Greek and Roman tales, are full of humans turning into creatures – lions, bears, donkeys. And fairy tales give us people turning into frogs, wolves, ugly beasts and back again.'

Johnny yawned.

'It all sounds silly, doesn't it? I mean, you are what you are. No one changes into anything, do they? But what if I tell you, Johnny' – he appeared by Johnny's side and made him jump – 'that you are pretty much a different person than the one you were a few years ago? Your cells have a finite lifespan and are replaced when they get old. Your skeleton will regenerate every seven years, your skin every few days. So, with some exceptions, very little remains from eight-year-old you.'

Johnny looked down at himself. The teacher couldn't be right. He looked the same. Just taller.

Anyway, he didn't want to be a different person. He liked who he had been then. A lot more than he liked who he was now.

'Because, much like Dr Who,' the teacher went on, 'our bodies regenerate, and they also change.'

The teacher moved back to the board and Johnny sunk into his chair, relieved that his chances of being picked on again – in this class, at least – were now close to zero.

The teacher was still talking. 'But something else, something even more amazing, is happening to you all. Can anyone tell me what it is?'

Embarrassed silence.

'Anyone?'

Even more embarrassed silence.

'OK, I'll tell you. It's *puberty*.'

He practically shouted the word, and everyone groaned. Johnny put his head on the desk.

'Puberty is a miraculous occurrence that is transforming you from your child state into your adult state. Without the aid of wicked witches' curses, magic potions or intervention from the divine, you are all transforming. Now you can open your books at page fifty-six, and let's look at just how this miracle happens.'

At lunchtime Johnny wondered if he would be safe in the canteen, but decided not to take the risk.

He waited until the whole class, including the teacher, had gone out. Then he let himself into the resources cupboard and sat in the dark among paper, pens and sex education books to eat his lunch.

Knowing he was in danger hadn't spoilt his appetite, and he'd just eaten half a sandwich and opened his crisps when he heard voices.

He peered through the keyhole and saw a group of Year Ten girls sitting on the tables and getting food out of their bags.

He could see the clock on the wall behind them. The *Swan Lake* rehearsal was in fifteen minutes, and he was worried that if he missed it he would be back on litter-picking duty. But he was stuck there until they left, so he sat down again and carried on eating, sucking his crisps until they went soft so they didn't make a noise, and listening to the girls' conversation.

'So, yeah, I was, like, no way. And he said, "You get it into me by three o'clock or you won't be doing that exam."' The girl sniffed and blew her nose.

'Don't worry, Lauren, you can copy mine,' another voice said.

There was silence, then he heard the first one say, 'You're the best.'

Johnny thought back to when he had friends who would have helped him out and not left him to hide in a cupboard to avoid being beaten up. Ronnie and Tagor, and Yusuf and Will. They would have made sure that no one touched him. But he hadn't seen any of them since he moved. Even though they'd said they would visit.

His crisps were finished now, so Johnny took out his apple and rubbed it on his trouser leg.

The girls were talking about a boy and giggling.

'I know, it's weird, isn't it, cos he's so small, but there's something about him that makes me go . . .'

Johnny heard giggles.

'I might ask him out.'

'You can't – he's only a Year Nine!'

'Yeah, but he's really mature.'

Johnny bit into his apple. It was a very hard green one and the crunch reverberated around the tiny space.

'What was that?'

'It's from in there.'

'D'you think it's a ghost?'

The girl nearest stood up and walked over.

Johnny held on to the door handle to stop it from turning.

'It's stuck.'

'Is someone in there?'

Johnny held his breath.

The girls sat back down.

He breathed out.

Then he heard the classroom door open.

'Afternoon, laydeez.'

Johnny put his eye to the keyhole again.

It was Liam Clark.

'You haven't seen the Swan Boy anywhere, have you?'

'No,' they said, giggling.

Then one added, 'Wouldn't tell you if we did, you bully.'

Liam walked out and they all laughed again.

Johnny grabbed the door handle and opened it.

One of the girls screamed.

'Hey, you're the Swan Boy! What were you doing in there?'

'Just reading,' he said, holding up a sex education book.

They all laughed.

'Liam Clark's looking for you, you know.'

'That's why I was hiding in a cupboard,' he said. 'Will you do me a favour?'

Hidden in the middle of the group of girls, Johnny was delivered safely to the changing room.

'Thanks. I owe you,' he said.

They laughed.

Johnny wondered why they found him so hysterical, but at least they were nice.

Stefan was already there. Even though they didn't like each other much, Johnny was glad that he had decided to do it too.

Stefan nodded at Johnny, and the pair got changed into their PE kits in silence.

Johnny had just pulled his T-shirt over his head when the door swung open and Liam walked in.

Johnny stood up, bracing himself. Was he going to get beaten up now? Just before the rehearsal?

But Liam didn't even look at him. His eyes were on Stefan.

'You got the money?'

Stefan looked down and mumbled, 'I can't this week.'

Liam's jaw jutted out and he drew himself up to his full, not particularly tall, height. He swore at Stefan, then spat, 'Double next week then. And no excuses.'

Stefan rubbed his huge hands through his greasy hair. 'I'll get it if I can, but it's not easy any more.'

'Double,' repeated Liam. Then he turned to Johnny. 'I haven't forgotten about you either,' he said and walked out of the room.

'Nice,' said Johnny. 'He's taking money off you?'

Stefan shrugged.

'How much?'

He was silent for a moment, then said in a small voice, 'Just a fiver a week.'

Johnny raised his eyebrows. A fiver a week was decent pocket money. More than he got, especially recently.

'So what's the problem?' he asked Stefan.

Stefan glared at him, then sighed. 'I've been getting it out of the till at my dad's pizza place.'

'Your dad's got a pizza place? Lucky you.'

'Yeah. Pete's Pizzas on Fellows Road. D'you know it?'

Johnny did know it. They'd been there once for a treat. 'Yeah, you do really good garlic bread.'

Stefan smiled. 'Dad says it's the best in town.'

'So, I've got to ask, what exactly does Liam do in return for his payment? Not beat you up?'

'Pretty much.' Stefan sighed. 'He's supposed to stop the others too.'

Johnny remembered the incident in registration.

As if Stefan could read his mind, he said, 'Yeah. It's not really working. Anyway, my dad won't let me near the till since he caught me a few weeks ago. He's got me in the back now, grating cheese, so it's pretty hard to get my hands on a fiver, let alone a tenner.'

'Pay him in mozzarella?'

Stefan laughed.

'Or how about you just don't pay?' said Johnny. 'Say no. What's he going to do?'

'He's gonna beat me up,' said Stefan. 'Obviously.'

'He's going to beat me up too,' said Johnny. 'So what? At least it's free.'

Stefan smiled. 'You're new here. You don't know what he's like, do you?'

Johnny shrugged. 'He's tiny. Maybe you could sit on him?'

Stefan shook his head. 'He might be small but Jonas isn't. He's like a bodybuilder, and Lola's vicious. They're both with him the whole time.'

Johnny stood up. 'Well, maybe you'd better pay then. And maybe I'd better stay out of his way too, because I don't like our chances against the three of them.'

'Our chances?' repeated Stefan. He stood up too and walked to the door. 'You're on your own, mate. I don't need more trouble in my life. And you, with all that swan stuff, you seem like trouble to me.'

Johnny shook his head. People at this school were so quick to judge.

He let Stefan go out first, then left the changing room and went into the gym.

'Ah, my Prince!' Mrs Cray said. 'Come in, come in. You're late – everyone else is already here. We only have two weeks until the performance and an awful lot to do.'

Johnny looked around. There were just one girl and four boys, including him and Stefan.

'But there's hardly anyone here,' he said. 'Aren't you gonna cancel it?'

Just then the door banged open.

'Welcome! Welcome!' said Mrs Cray.

Eight more kids came in, all carrying high-vis vests and long orange-handled rubbish pickers, which they threw in a clattering heap.

Last to trail in were Liam and his friends. Johnny's heart started pounding. He knew that Liam wouldn't hurt him there, in front of the teacher, but he couldn't keep control of his fear.

Mrs Cray, on the other hand, was beaming.

'A change of heart?' she asked them.

'The caretaker wanted us to wear these too!' A Year Seven showed her a peaked cap with *TEAM TIDY* printed on it. 'I have my limits,' he added.

'Well, you're all very welcome here,' said Mrs Cray. 'And I won't make you wear anything luminous.'

No, Johnny thought, *but probably something with feathers.*

Mrs Cray reached into a patchwork bag and took out a flyer. She held it up.

'Look, Johnny. What do you think?'

It was *Swan Lake* all right.

But no tutus or ballet shoes. There were real swans, muscular and majestic, flying across the page.

Johnny could almost imagine it. Then he remembered that it was going to be *them* doing the dancing.

He looked at the other boys, a few of them still struggling with their own shoelaces or getting their heads stuck in their jumpers, and he thought about the grace and the power of the swans.

'But how?' He had meant to think it, but the words had slipped out. 'How are *we* going to do a ballet?'

Mrs Cray pursed her lips. 'Well,' she said, 'it won't be strictly ballet. Not how you're imagining it. It will be more free, like modern dance.'

Behind her, the boys were now goofing around, trying to trip each other up.

'And we will be doing it in our own way. Just four short scenes and none of the very technical moves. But, yes, it's an ambitious project.'

'I don't think we can do it,' Johnny said. 'Sorry, but you've seen that lot? I reckon we'll just end up looking stupid.'

She smiled at him, and the lines around her eyes squeezed together into a fan. 'But what if we pull it off, Johnny? What if it's a triumph?'

He knew that wasn't the sort of question that required an answer. And she wouldn't have liked his answer anyway.

'So,' she addressed the whole group, 'every journey starts with a few steps, and today we're going to take ours. We have lots of wonderful swans, so we just need to decide who's playing the Queen, and who's the girlfriend, and our cast will be complete.'

'Liam Clark in a wig?' Johnny muttered.

Mrs Cray looked over towards Liam. He was standing in his footie shorts, surrounded by his friends, scowling, with his arms folded. He looked small and skinny, and it was hard to believe that anyone was scared of him.

'I was joking!' Johnny said.

'I know, but I've just had an idea.' Mrs Cray raised her voice. 'Liam, come here, I need to ask you something.'

He frowned, but walked over.

'Liam, I have a special role for you. I've noticed that you have certain . . . leadership qualities.'

Liam stuck his chest out and almost smiled.

'The role I want you to take on requires a person with natural authority. You are to be the Black Swan, the head of the flock.'

Liam looked over at his friends, then back at Mrs Cray. 'Head Swan?'

'That's right. And the others will be your flock.'

'So, I'm a swan, and they're all my team? And they have to do what I say?'

'Yes. Everyone except for Johnny, Stefan and the girls.'

He scowled. 'You're not gonna make me look stupid, are you?'

Mrs Cray's eyes opened wide and she shook her head. 'Oh no. No, no, no, Liam. I would never do that. I will make you look magnificent.'

Liam shrugged his shoulders. 'OK. I'll do it, I s'pose.'

'You won't be sorry,' said Mrs Cray, smiling.

Johnny couldn't believe it. Liam was a bully and the whole school knew it, but Mrs Cray was rewarding him for it?

When Johnny did something wrong he just got in trouble. The things that happened in his last school, just after his dad died, they weren't all that serious: a bit of bunking off, answering his teachers back, lying for his mates. He had never hurt anyone. But he got a bad reputation and punishments. Not a reward for his independent thinking, communication skills and creativity.

'OK, everyone in your places. We've got work to do!' Mrs Cray put on the music. 'Boys, remember that we may be using ballet steps, but I want to see *masculinity*! Boys must dance like boys, do you understand? OK, first let's get the blood flooding to your biceps and pectorals with twenty press-ups!'

66

Only a few of them managed it, but the press-ups were followed by twenty squats.

Stefan was red-faced and panting. 'Miss, can we stop now?' he asked.

'Yes,' she said. 'Now, who wants to learn to sword fight?'

A cheer went up, followed by a groan when they realised that they would be using imaginary swords.

Mrs Cray showed the group how to lunge and thrust, and then they started practising in pairs.

Stefan, shining with sweat, came and stood next to Johnny.

'You wanna go together?'

Johnny shrugged. 'All right.'

They moved to the edge of the group, well away from Liam.

'*En garde!*' Johnny shouted and attacked him.

'*En garde*, yourself!' Stefan responded, slicing his head off.

Johnny answered with a blow to his chest.

'You can't do that. You were dead,' Stefan said.

Johnny shook his head. 'It's just a game. Don't be weird about it.'

'I'm not,' said Stefan. 'You're not being fair though.'

'Go with someone else if you don't like it.'

On the other side of the room, Liam Clark was pinning down a small boy and repeatedly stabbing him with his imaginary sword.

'Nah, you're all right,' Stefan said. '*En garde!*'

Mrs Cray clapped her hands for attention.

'My brave musketeers!' she said. 'You are without doubt potentially the most talented young dancers with whom I have had the pleasure of working. Today you

67

have shown me strength, enthusiasm, valour and, with a few exceptions, grace under fire – qualities seen in all the best corps de ballet. So I'm now 100% convinced that the show will be a big . . . no, an *enormous* success.'

Someone yawned loudly, and Liam started chatting to Lola.

'First, some practicalities. We will only have the school hall for an hour on the day, so sadly we won't be able to tackle the full show, but that doesn't mean that we can't distil the essence of the story – the passion, the beauty and, ultimately, the tragic death – and use it in our own interpretation.'

A few kids looked up at the mention of death.

'And now we will sort out roles. Johnny, you're Prince Siegfried, whose life is stifling and miserable, and whose goal it is to become like the beautiful swans. Stefan, you're Von Rothbart, the evil sorcerer who wants to get rid of the Prince so that he can rule the land in his place. Lola, you're the Prince's would-be-girl-friend. Phoebe, who has kindly offered to join us to make up numbers, you're the Prince's mother. Liam, you're the Black Swan, the son of the evil sorcerer. The rest of you are courtiers in the first scene, and after that you're my beautiful flock of swans.'

Mrs Cray looked around, her eyes resting on Johnny. 'If our *Swan Lake* is to succeed, you must take your roles seriously. Live, breathe and become your part. Now, divide yourselves into three groups.'

A few people muttered about being swans, but, with the Team Tidy vests still illuminating the corner of the gym, they gathered into small groups.

'So, let's get started,' said Mrs Cray. 'Spread yourselves out. Johnny, you come to the front. Scene one. Setting:

the palace. Johnny, you're the very unhappy, young Prince trying to live up to the Queen's expectations, but you keep making mistakes.'

'What do you mean, expectations?'

'Well, the Queen is grooming you to be King, but you're not ready to take on the responsibilities of royal life yet. You're still young. You don't want to be restricted.'

Johnny knew that feeling:

Pick up Mojo.

Cook dinner.

Clear up Mojo's mess.

Wash up.

Clean the flat.

Stay in.

Be responsible.

Be a man.

Be boring.

All without the advantages of being a prince.

Mrs Cray interrupted his thoughts. 'I'm glad to see that expression on your face, Johnny. It's exactly the one I need. Show us your frustration, your anger.'

Johnny had spent months trying to keep his feelings inside. He wasn't about to show anybody anything. Nothing real anyway.

'And, Phoebe, you're his mother. It's your job to mould him so that he can fulfil his destiny. From this boy you must create a great king who can rule your lands after you're gone.'

Mrs Cray called out to the other kids, 'Courtiers, you're going to be in charge of training the young Prince in his duties. Your first task is to teach him to bow properly.'

Mrs Cray raised herself to her full height before bowing so low that her face touched her knees.

'Now you try, Johnny,' she said. 'But I don't want good. I want you to do it wrong at first.'

'Wrong?'

'Yes, do it badly.'

'OK,' he said.

He felt confident that he could do it wrong and he tried a quick bow, more like a bob.

'No, too good,' she said. 'I want worse. I want clumsy and unregal.'

Johnny couldn't believe that he had even messed up getting something wrong, but he thought a moment, then stuck his foot out and stumbled as he bowed.

Mrs Cray clapped her hands together. 'Excellently terrible!' she said. 'Now add this.' She copied what Johnny had done, but added in some dance steps.

Johnny repeated it without thinking. Without feeling either. Just letting himself get carried along by Mrs Cray's orders.

'Courtiers, group one: your Prince's bow is a mess. Please teach him to bow properly.'

'Can we hit him if he gets it wrong?' someone asked.

Mrs Cray smiled. 'You can appear to punish him, but no actual contact is allowed.'

They stood around arguing about how to do it then they modelled it, just as Mrs Cray had done, and changed Johnny's position, pretending to beat him when he stumbled. Mrs Cray then gave them some steps and funny arm movements to include, which they repeated until Johnny was bowing correctly.

'That will do. Well done. Courtiers, group two: deportment.'

Mrs Cray got the second group to teach Johnny to walk regally, his head held high as if there were a crown on it.

'But I might trip up on something,' Johnny said.

'You won't,' Mrs Cray told him. 'You're a prince looking forward to being a king. Don't concern yourself with anything at your feet.'

Johnny started walking, following the others, slouching at first, then finally straightening himself up and gazing into the distance.

As he did, he felt his shoulders drop and his breathing slow. It took him away from the school gymnasium to somewhere else. Somewhere better.

'That's great. Carry on like that,' said Mrs Cray as she went to change the music.

Johnny was aware of someone laughing, but he was focused on a spot just out of view.

He didn't even hear the ball as it rolled towards him. The first he knew of it was that he kicked it as he walked.

It broke the spell.

A disappointed 'Ohhh . . .' came from the room.

He looked round.

Liam was smirking.

He'd tried to bowl him over.

But he had failed.

Johnny allowed himself a small smile.

Mrs Cray came back. 'Right then. Courtiers, group three: waving from the royal carriage.'

Johnny's smile disappeared as he realised that this was Jonas's group.

Mrs Cray held out a stool. 'Johnny, you stand on this. Group three, stand around him and move your arms as if they're wheels.'

Johnny climbed up on the stool, and the group sloped over and gathered round him.

'OK, let's see those wheels spinning!'

71

The group began to make a turning motion with their arms.

'Now, Johnny, you must wave, but badly at first.'

In time with the rising music, the wheels spun, while Johnny waved like an excited three-year-old. He was just pleased that Jonas was at the front and couldn't see him looking so stupid.

'Lovely,' said Mrs Cray. 'Now, Lola, come and correct the Prince's waving.'

Lola stood up, grabbed Johnny's arm and yanked it around.

Johnny grabbed his arm back. 'Oy, that hurts!'

Mrs Cray clapped her hands together. 'That was brilliant! Do it just like that every time! Right, let's take it from the top.'

She went to change the music again, and Liam came over.

'Did you touch my girlfriend, Swan Boy?'

Liam put his hand out, grabbed Johnny's shorts and pulled at them. Johnny lost his balance, and, just as Mrs Cray turned back, he fell off the stool with his shorts around his ankles.

The room exploded into laughter.

'Johnny!' said Mrs Cray. 'Please don't start clowning around. This story is a tragedy, not a comedy.'

Liam was grinning and wagging his finger at him.

Everyone was laughing along with him – and at Johnny.

He didn't get it. What made him so funny?

He didn't feel funny at all.

He felt furious.

He felt like punching that smile right off Liam's face.

He looked down at his clenched fists. His hands had never been used like that. And he wasn't sure he wanted to start.

Anyway, he knew he would never win, so there was no point in even trying.

Mrs Cray clapped to get their attention. 'Class, you have been brilliant. Same time on Thursday, and remember to practise your steps at home.'

She turned to Johnny. 'A word, please, before you go, my Prince?'

Then she set a different piece of music to play, strong and powerful, the whole orchestra taking the melody that he had heard earlier and turning it into something huge and emotional and triumphant.

Johnny, though, felt small and embarrassed and defeated as he shuffled over, waiting to be told off about the shorts incident.

But Mrs Cray was smiling at him. 'Johnny, there's something I want you to practise for a scene at the end. I was unsure whether to give it to you or to Liam, but, as your little joke just now shows, you're brave enough to take a few risks.'

His little joke? Johnny opened his mouth to speak, to tell her that it was Liam, but she was still talking.

'It's a very special leap, and the only technically difficult piece of ballet that we'll be including, so it has to be really impressive.'

'A leap?' he said. He was about to add, *I don't want to do anything hard. Give it to Liam – make him look like an idiot instead*, when she walked away from him.

'Look, I'll show you.'

She stood in one corner of the gym and he couldn't really imagine how she was going to get her thick, middle-aged body off the floor. But, after a few quick hard steps that made the wooden floor vibrate under his feet, Mrs Cray launched herself into the air.

It must have taken less than a second, but the shape that she made burnt into his retina like the sun.

Her right leg was stretched straight out in front. Her left was bent gently behind her. One arm was held slightly to the side; the other was pointing straight up.

It was almost like she was doing the splits in the air.

She didn't look human any more.

She was flying.

Actually flying.

And he wanted to do it too.

'Go on, then. You have a go,' she said. 'Shoulders down, long neck and use the stage.'

Johnny started from the same place, running diagonally across the gym. When he reached the middle, he jumped as high and wide as he could, throwing his front leg out and leaving his back leg trailing.

It was over so soon, and his leap hadn't felt anything like Mrs Cray's had looked. He hadn't *changed* as he jumped like she had. He had been himself, but half a metre off the ground.

He was ashamed that he had even tried.

'It wasn't terrible,' said Mrs Cray.

'Give it to Liam,' he said. 'I can't do it.'

She smiled and shook her head. 'No, it's yours. Just keep practising. You'll get it if you want it enough.'

'I don't want it. I can't do it – I'd ruin the show. I'm sorry,' he said, and he walked out of the gym.

As he opened the changing-room door, Liam Clark and his mates were bundling out, laughing.

Liam glared at him, then Jonas slammed Johnny into the door frame with his shoulder.

'Nice undies,' Jonas said, winking at him.

Stefan was sitting on the bench.

'What did Mrs Cray-Cray want?' he asked.

Johnny shrugged. 'Just telling me off about Liam pulling down my shorts.'

Stefan laughed. 'You've gotta admit that was funny.'

Johnny narrowed his eyes. 'Hilarious.'

'Did you know it was *Swan Lake*?' Stefan said. 'Ballet,' he added, in case Johnny didn't know what it was.

Johnny sat down next to him. 'Yeah.'

'I don't really care,' Stefan said. 'I like dancing. I'm better at dancing than I am at football. But it doesn't exactly make you popular in the same way.'

Johnny snorted. 'Not exactly, no. Anyway, I think I'm going to do the litter pick after all. It's got to be better than this.'

'Why?' said Stefan. 'This is just a few rehearsals, then a show that no one will come to. The litter pick is a whole month of hell.' He grabbed his bag. 'Right, I'm off. Laters, taters,' he said and walked out.

Alone in the changing room, Johnny thought about the leap again.

How graceful Mrs Cray was.

How useless he was.

As he got back into his uniform and packed his PE kit into his bag, he couldn't stop thinking about that leap. Mrs Cray had made it look so easy.

It might be too late – maybe she had already given it to Liam – but he decided that he should try it one more time.

Johnny walked to the very end of the room. It wasn't really big enough, but he had to try.

He took a quick run-up and leapt.

He had barely left the ground when his back leg hit one of the lockers and he crashed into a bench.

'Ha! Ha!'

Liam Clark was standing at the door. Behind him were Jonas and Lola.

Liam clapped slowly three times.

'Laters, taters,' he said, smirking.

Johnny now knew two things. Firstly, Liam had been standing there the whole time, spying on him and Stefan. And secondly, the shorts incident was just for starters – Liam was still intending to beat him up.

Chapter Six

The final lesson of the day was double English. They were studying a book that Johnny had done at his last school, so he wasn't really listening.

'Wakey-wakey, Johnny!' Suddenly Mr Radley was wheezing mint and bad breath over him. 'Maybe you could tell us what you think Boxer, the horse in *Animal Farm*, represents?'

'Erm . . .' Johnny knew the answer; it was on the tip of his tongue.

'I thought you must know,' the teacher continued, in a sarcastic tone, 'and that's why you decided it was a good time to nap.'

Johnny tried desperately to remember, to show the teacher that he wasn't stupid.

'Come on, Johnny. Please enlighten us.'

'Erm . . .'

There was a timid knock at the door.

'Enter!' Even the teacher looked relieved at the interruption.

A Year Seven, who was barely strong enough to push the door open, came in with a note.

The teacher read it, then frowned.

'You can tell us next time, Johnny. Apparently you're needed at home urgently, so pack up and leave quietly.'

Johnny froze. The sound of his own blood was pumping in his ears. Something had happened to his mum or Mojo. It had to be them. Why else would he be called out of school urgently?

He threw everything into his bag and ran out of the classroom. Then he scribbled a few lopsided letters from his name into the signing-out book at the reception.

As he reached the heavy front doors, a teacher appeared on the other side of the glass. He was escorting Lola and Jonas back in, and none of them looked happy.

Johnny barged through, receiving glares from all three, but he didn't care. He was already at maximum anxiety, his fears screaming like a choir of maniacs in his head, dread dragging his guts down with every step.

Then his knees began to lock. It was like a dream where he was being chased but had forgotten how to run.

While he battled with his coordination, the 'what ifs' were playing, like a racing commentary, in his head.

What if Mojo was hurt?

What if Mum was hurt?

What if one of them was dead?

What if they were both dead?

What if he was alone now?

Completely alone?

He had to calm down.

He had to be strong.

He remembered the roof swan. He put his hand into his bag and took its feather out. It was a bit squashed, but he concentrated on the feel of it, light and delicate but tough and smooth.

It calmed him. His legs loosened up, and he managed to break into a jog, leaving the school grounds and the main road behind, and running round the corner towards home.

He had his head down so he didn't notice that someone was blocking his way until he nearly ran into him.

Liam Clark.

Liam's face was taut, his bottom jaw jutting out; he looked pumped up and ready to attack. But when he saw the feather, Liam's expression changed and he took a step backwards.

'What're you carrying that for?' His voice was higher than Johnny was expecting.

Johnny looked down at the swan's feather. 'Nothing. Let me past. I've gotta get home. It's an emergency.'

Liam shuffled his feet. If Johnny hadn't known better, he would have said that Liam Clark was nervous.

'There, er . . . There is no emergency. I, er, I set it up so I could get you on your own.'

Johnny exhaled, smoothing down the feather.

His mum was OK.

Mojo was OK.

Everything was OK.

And then the anger rose in him. He clenched his fists.

'What did you do that for?'

Liam shrugged, looking past Johnny's shoulder, and the desire to hit him became almost unbearable.

Then a smile spread across Liam's face, and when he spoke his voice had changed, a hard edge replacing the nerves.

'I think you know what for. You made me look like an idiot with that bird. Then you went and got us all in trouble with your library stunt. And now you reckon you're so special cos you've got the lead part in some pathetic dance show. You make me sick.'

Liam's eyes flicked past Johnny again.

What was he looking at?

Johnny spun around just in time to see Jonas and Lola running towards them. He realised too late that turning his back on Liam had been a mistake, as Liam grabbed him round the neck and pushed him down on to the ground.

With his face close to the concrete, all that Johnny could see were Liam's dirty shoes crushing the feather. He put his hand out to grab it and Liam stamped hard on his knuckles.

The other two were getting closer, shouting, 'Swaaan Boy!' at the top of their voices. It was like a war cry.

'Get off!' Johnny was shouting, but he knew that he was beaten. Even if he managed to get away from Liam, the others would catch him.

He shut his eyes and raised his arms to protect his head as Jonas and Lola arrived, and all three attacked.

First someone's shoe hit the side of his head.

'Stop, please!' Johnny shouted. 'I'm sorry!'

Then a harder kick came crashing from the other side into his ribcage.

'I'm sorry about the swan,' he said. 'And the library. I'm sorry about it all!'

'Not sorry enough,' Liam replied.

Hands pulled him up to a sitting position, and he knew that he should fight back, but he wasn't strong enough.

Then he felt a blow to the centre of his chest.

And he couldn't breathe.

He couldn't breathe at all.

Where there should have been the in–out sing-song of his lungs, the music of his own body, there was nothing.

Silence.

Was he going to die?

Was this it?

Would he never see Mum and Mojo again?

He had to start his music again.

But he didn't know how.

Then he heard it. A rhythm, but not his own. There were muffled notes too, like the sound of a marching band in the distance.

'What's happened to him?' The voice sounded distorted, like someone talking through a tube.

'He's a funny colour.'

'Get up, Swan Boy!'

There was a tug on his arm.

The music rose, drowning out the voices.

'Stop faking!'

But it wasn't his music.

It was rhythmic, but complicated and beautiful.

He had heard it before.

Swan Lake.

It was the music from *Swan Lake.*

It was rising and swelling, and he made his body follow what it was doing, forcing his lungs to breathe in and out along with it.

'He's definitely faking,' Lola said.

The music was roaring now, her voice just a whisper.

'All right, he's learnt his lesson.'

That was Liam.

'Let's get out of here before anyone sees us.'

Johnny listened to their footsteps retreating, then he opened his eyes and carefully sat up.

His head spinning, he checked himself over.

His knuckles were skinned where Liam had trodden on them, and he was tender, particularly on his chest where he had been kicked, but he was going to be OK.

He knew he had to start moving, so he stood up slowly. But where to go? Definitely not back to school. But it was too early to pick up Mojo, and too late to go home first.

He found himself walking towards Primrose Hill. He would go there to clean up in the public toilets.

A uniformed attendant stared at him as he walked in.

'You all right, son?' He had a thick Scottish accent. 'Do you want me to call someone?'

'No. I just slipped.'

'But shouldn't you be in school?'

'No, I, er, I've been to a clarinet exam.'

The man sat back down and picked up his newspaper.

'Well, if you change your mind . . .'

In front of the mirror Johnny washed his hands, face and hair as well as he could, then he inspected his injuries.

A large foot-shaped bruise was blooming grey on his chest, but his face was unmarked. They had kicked him from the side, so most of the bruising was hidden by his hair.

'Take care,' the man said as Johnny limped out.

Little children were shrieking in the play park. It was Mojo's favourite place – in fact, it was almost the only place he had seemed happy since they moved house.

Johnny walked across the road and past the zoo, into Regent's Park and around the top of the lake. The path was high above the water, and in the distance he could see the bright blue pedalos tethered together, waiting for tourists.

Tables and chairs were sprawled outside the cafe, and, as he came closer, he saw mothers drinking coffee and toddlers sucking lollies. He felt disapproval in their glances and hurried past as fast as he could, despite his injuries, keeping his head down, facing his feet.

He didn't stop until he reached the spot where he had sat on the school trip.

It was a wide expanse of short-cut lawn where the lake lapped the shore. The grass was the same – dotted with cigarette butts, splattered with bird droppings and scorched with rectangles from picnickers' barbecues – and there was the sign that banned almost every activity except for morris dancing.

A small island stuck up from the middle of the lake, with some sort of mouldy birdhouse on it. Behind it was an area that was roped off to stop the pedalos, with a large *DANGER – KEEP OUT* sign attached. To the other side was a larger island accessible by a footbridge, and a sign pointing the way to the Open Air Theatre.

Johnny crouched by the edge of the water. It was a greenish grey where it met the shore and it left a dark, unhealthy stain on the concrete.

Bobbing on the surface were tiny plants that looked like cress and dead brown leaves. Curled white feathers were suspended in a layer of scum.

Worst of all, there were no swans. Just a few moorhens and great ugly geese looking his way, hoping for a crust.

Johnny went back to sit on a bench facing the lake, wondering what he was doing there. A cloud passed in front of the June sun, and he shivered.

Then he felt a nudging on his trouser leg. He looked down and there was a little white dog.

Johnny put his hand out. 'Hello.'

The dog sniffed the air around him.

'Fifi, come away.'

Its owner, in high-heeled boots and a shimmering pearl raincoat, frowned at him, before going back to her phone conversation.

The dog looked Johnny in the eyes then started sniffing his shoes, working its way up to his pocket.

'I haven't got anything for you. Look.'

He put his hand in and felt the feather. The one that Liam had stamped on. He didn't even remember picking it up.

The dog sat back, its tail sweeping the ground and a hopeful expression on its little face.

'You want this?' he asked the dog.

Johnny stroked the feather.

'Not really sure why I kept it in the first place. It's all a bit weird,' he said out loud. 'Here, have it.'

The dog gently took the feather in its mouth then tipped its head upwards. Its pupils reflected the pale blue of the sky, before filling with white.

Johnny looked up too then. Seven swans were heading towards them. The sound of their wings beating away the air made his body tingle.

As they came nearer they formed an arrow shape, with a leader in front like a tip, and three on either side making its shaft. The swan arrow was pointing straight at the lake.

'You came!' he said softly. 'You knew I was here and you . . .'

But the swans weren't slowing or descending.

'No! Come back!'

As they passed right overhead he could almost feel the pull of the air above him. But Johnny wasn't disappointed any more. He wanted to cry with happiness.

A park ranger in a moss-green uniform looked up from the leaves he was sweeping. 'Impressive, aren't they?'

Johnny nodded. 'Where are they going? Are they migrating?'

'No, they're stuck in London all year round, just like us.'

He finished sweeping his leaves into a neat pile and walked off, and Johnny realised that the little dog was still sitting at his feet.

'Drop,' he said, and the dog opened its mouth and let the damp feather fall out, then ran off in the direction of its owner.

Johnny stroked the feather, smoothing the barbs back into place.

He held it tight as he limped all the way to Mojo's school.

Lily Simpson had blonde hair that curled like bedsprings, and all Mojo had wanted to do was to push his finger through a ringlet and see what it felt like.

But when she had reached over for the glue, his fingers had got caught and she had screamed, which made Mojo panic and grip the ringlet tight.

His teacher prised his hand open, one glittery finger at a time. Mojo tried to tell her that he didn't like the sound of screaming, that it had made him scared, and his mind had gone blank and that's why he couldn't let go.

But she didn't listen.

'That's three sad-face clouds today, Mojo,' she said, standing what felt like a mile above him, and pointing to the naughty corner of the whiteboard, where his name sat alone. 'And not a single smiley sun.'

The good side of the board was crowded with the names of the nice children.

'You know what that means, don't you?'

The corridor that led to the head teacher's office was decorated in brightly coloured pictures done by the other children at the school. Not the ones who had to sit in the head teacher's office and be told off.

The chair opposite the head teacher was too tall, so Mojo's legs dangled and his feet started to feel fuzzy. But from there he could at least see all the interesting things on his desk: the back of the picture frame, the big stapler and a glass paperweight with blue swirls in it like an eye.

'Mojo,' the head teacher said, 'do you like it in here with me?'

He had wavy grey hair and, though his smile was hidden by a beard, Mojo could see it in his eyes.

'Yes,' said Mojo.

'But wouldn't you prefer to be with everyone else in the classroom?'

Mojo frowned. 'No, it's too loud and children-y. I can't think.'

The head teacher laughed. 'Well, maybe that's why punishing you by bringing you here isn't working too well.' He picked up the phone. 'Miss Johnson, could you send someone to take Mojo back. From now on I think it's best if he stays in the classroom.'

Mojo grabbed the glass paperweight, pulled back his arm and threw it as hard as he could at the window.

The teacher was gripping Mojo by the shoulders when Johnny arrived to pick him up.

'We haven't had a very good day,' the teacher said. 'We tried to call your mother, but she was in a meeting, so could you give her this letter, please?'

Johnny took the narrow white envelope.

PRIVATE AND CONFIDENTIAL was printed on the front in red ink.

'I'll pass it on,' he said, and reached for his brother's hand.

Mojo's eyes were angry and red to match the lettering.

'What happened?' Johnny asked as they walked away.

'Nothing,' said Mojo.

'It didn't sound like nothing.'

He sighed. 'I'm on the cloud again.'

'Because of whatever's written in here?'

Mojo said, 'I don't know what's written in there.'

'But can you guess?'

Mojo thought, then nodded. 'And I have to stay on the cloud all week.'

They were off the school grounds now, so Johnny opened the letter and read it quickly.

He whistled. 'Did you really break the window?'

Mojo nodded. 'Yes, but don't tell Mum. It was an accident. The glass thing flew out of my hand. It was slippy.'

'I dunno, Moj. This is bad. I mean, you could've hurt someone.'

Mojo sniffed. 'I said sorry. I just want to be on the sunny side of the board again, like everyone else.'

Johnny put his arm around Mojo's shoulders and squeezed him. 'OK, I won't tell her. But she'll probably find out anyway.'

Mojo gave him a watery smile. 'Thank you. I won't do it again. I'll be really good for ever and ever now.'

Johnny laughed. 'Well, I think for ever is a long time, but how about being really good for the rest of the week?'

Mojo nodded. 'Yes. 'Til Friday. I'll be good 'til Friday.'

★ ★ ★

Back at the flat, Johnny hid the letter under his bed, then lay on the sofa in front of the TV while Mojo drew on the table.

At half past five he heard the front door open.

'Tea, love?' Mum called through to the living room.

'Please.'

A minute later she appeared with two mugs and set one down on the coffee table next to him.

Then she screamed.

He leapt up, looking around him.

'What? What is it?'

She was shaking her head at him. 'What have you done, Johnny?'

'Nothing! I was just watching telly.'

'No.' She moved towards him with her hand out. 'I mean your hair!'

'Oh, that. It's probably a bit of dirt. I got some mud in it at school.'

But she was still staring. 'Your hair, Johnny! Your hair! Why on earth would you do that to your lovely hair?'

'What are you talking about?'

He got up and went into the bathroom. Standing in front of the mirror, waiting for the gloomy light to come on properly, he could see it already.

A thick white streak through the front of his black hair.

Mojo was standing in the doorway. 'You look like a badger,' he said. 'What noise does a badger make?'

Johnny went closer to the mirror. The streak was the width of his thumb and dazzling white from the roots to the tips. He ran his hands through and gave it a gentle tug.

'I don't understand,' he said. 'I was normal about an hour ago.'

'Has something happened today?' his mum asked.

He thought.

He'd been worried about being beaten up.

Mrs Cray had tried to teach him to fly.

He actually was beaten up.

He went to the park and the swans came.

He'd become the guardian of his brother's paperweight-chucking secret.

None of which he could tell his mum about.

'Nothing unusual,' he said.

A few minutes later, sitting round the kitchen table drinking their tea – his now with three sugars, hers with a drop of something for the shock – Mum said, 'We shouldn't really be surprised. Your grandfather on your dad's side had a white streak.'

'Did he?'

'Oh yes. Course it was white all over by the time I knew him, but I've seen the photos. I expect I've got one somewhere – I'll dig it out later. Anyway, it was just like yours. The family always said it appeared the day his house burnt down.' She leant back and looked at him. 'It's actually quite nice. Distinguished.'

Great.

'I don't want to be distinguished, Mum,' Johnny said. 'I'm thirteen. I want to be normal.'

She put her hand on his arm. 'I know, I know.'

Then she grinned and nudged him. 'Look on the bright side though – when you start going to pubs with your schoolmates, you'll be the only one that gets served.'

Johnny lowered his forehead to the table. It was probably his new 'mates' that were responsible for the white streak.

'I can't go to school tomorrow.' He spoke into the tablecloth.

'Why? Do you think you'll get teased?'

Johnny raised his head and stared at her.

'Er, yes, don't you?' he said, wondering how parents could be so ancient, and yet so innocent.

His mum fiddled with her wedding ring, turning it round and round. 'If you're really worried we can get some hair dye. I'll do my roots at the same time.'

'Before the morning?'

'Well, no, I can't manage that, I'm afraid. It's the sort of thing you have to go into town for.'

Johnny sighed loudly. 'Then you'll have to let me stay home.'

She shook her head. 'I can't do that either. I had a letter last week about your attendance. Twelve absences due to sickness, they reckon. Any more days off and we'll get a visit from the truant officer. The last thing I want is some- one poking their noses in, Johnny. I'm sorry.'

He looked at his mum and, just for a moment, he hated her.

'Thanks for nothing,' he said, and stamped the five steps to his room.

Johnny's school bag was lying on his bed, so he picked it up and flung it at the wall.

As it crashed down, *The Wildlife of Our Rivers and Lakes* flew on to the floor, and the middle pages fell out.

He picked them up and lay down on his bed. He was glad that Mojo wasn't there. He needed to be alone for a moment.

The room was so small that he could reach Mojo from his bed, and he could always hear him breathing at night. Sometimes Mojo whimpered and muttered weird things in his sleep. He hated that.

Johnny lay on his back and reread the page about swans.

They are fiercely protective of their young and have been known to break a person's arm in defence of their nests.

And something weird occurred to him.

Maybe the white streak had nothing to do with Liam Clark and his lot after all.

He thought about the dance lesson. Mrs Cray had told him to 'become' the part. And when he had seen her fly it had shaken him awake. It made him want to do something, to be something different.

Had he taken her literally? Was he trying to become a swan?

Then he groaned. He remembered that he had told Mrs Cray he wouldn't do it. He had told her to give the leap to Liam.

Liam, of all people!

He was an idiot.

He would tell her that he had changed his mind. He had to learn to do it.

He had to fly like a swan.

Lying on his saggy old bed in the tower block in London, he began to imagine what it would be like to be a swan, to have a long, muscular neck.

Without actually moving, he felt himself twisting and turning his head, and, as he did so, his neck seemed to get longer, stronger and dangerous, like a snake.

And when he had explored how it felt to have a long, flexible neck, his shoulders began to tingle, so he shrugged and wriggled them. Then the movement changed into a rhythmic beat and they suddenly felt heavier, and he knew that the action had unfolded wings from his shoulders.

He had wings. Big, heavy, strong wings.

Wings that could break a person's arm.

Wings that could carry him away.

'Johnny! Dinner's ready!'

He opened his eyes and he was back.

But the changes had felt so real. He checked his shoulders and ran his hand up and down his neck to make sure that he had imagined it.

Then he stood up and the reflection in the mirror on the wall told him that one change hadn't disappeared.

He took the swan's feather and lined it up with the streak in his hair. It matched perfectly.

His mum and Mojo were eating dinner on their laps in front of the TV.

'What do you want to watch, Johnny?' his mum asked. 'It's your choice tonight.'

Johnny flipped through the channels, but as they could no longer afford an expensive monthly package there wasn't much to choose from.

'Football?' he suggested.

His mum groaned. 'Really?'

'OK, how about *Behind the Scenes at Formula One*? I think it's a documentary.'

Mojo scowled. 'Looks boooooring.'

'A comedy?'

'Probably not suitable for Mojo.'

Johnny sighed.

'Look, Johnny, that emergency vet programme's good. We'll all like that, won't we?'

Johnny gave in. Even when it looked like he was being given a choice, he wasn't really.

They sat through half an hour of a vet's day, at the end of which the puppy they had all been rooting for died.

His mum wiped a tear from her eye and helped Mojo to blow his nose.

'Maybe next time I'll choose the programme, Johnny,' she said, as if it was his fault.

'You did,' he muttered.

'What was that?'

'Never mind.'

Later that night when they had gone to bed, Johnny heard his mum crying.

He put on his dressing gown and went into her room. She was sitting on her bed surrounded by old photographs.

'What is it?' he said. 'Is it the puppy? It probably didn't die really. They might have faked it to make the programme more interesting.'

She smiled through the tears.

'No, Johnny, it's not the puppy, though that was very sad. I was just . . .' She motioned towards the photos, and gave a hiccupy shudder. 'I was looking for one of your grandfather, and I found all these.'

She picked up a photo of his dad, with six-year-old Johnny on his shoulders. He looked so big and strong, like nothing could slay him.

'I miss him so much,' she said, the tears still flowing.

Johnny put his arms around his mum's neck and rested his head on hers.

'It'll be OK,' he said while she sobbed – like she was the child, not him.

Finally she stopped crying and blew her nose.

'I didn't manage to find it, sorry. The photo of your grandad.'

Johnny sat down next to her and she passed him an old Polaroid. A scene from a party when she was a teenager.

'Look at this one – your dad looks just like you there.'

Johnny glanced, then looked away. He didn't want to see it. He didn't want to compare their faces. If he recognised his face in his dad's, maybe he would see his dad's face in his own every time he looked in the mirror.

He pushed the photo to the bottom of the pile.

His dad had gone. Simple as that. He had left them, and Johnny's anger was managing to fill the nothingness where he used to be.

That was how he was coping.

Finding his dad again in his own face would only complicate things.

Chapter Seven

Wednesday

'You will go straight to school, won't you, Johnny?'

'Course I will.' Johnny couldn't help sounding annoyed. 'As long as you don't forget to bring back the hair dye like you said.'

'Deal,' his mum called out as he left the flat.

Once outside, Johnny crossed the road and looked up at the eighth-floor windows. His mum wasn't watching, so he turned left instead of right and, with no plan in his head, he just kept putting one foot in front of the other.

It was the first time that Johnny had skipped school since they had moved.

His mum had made him promise that he wouldn't do it any more, and he had kept his word. But the thing with the hair changed everything. Anyone could see that.

He felt a bit nervous – guilty, even. But gradually, as he walked, Johnny's stomach unknotted and he began to relax, and started to focus instead on the rhythm of his footsteps.

One–two, one–two, one–two.

Quickly the beat of his steps became hypnotic; he tuned out the street and the cars, the kids from his school

95

going in the opposite direction, and as he did so music started to play.

It was so quiet at first that he barely noticed it keeping time with his strides.

Then it became louder in his head, and it was as if he was wearing headphones, but better.

Instead of the sound coming in through his ears, he felt the surge of the orchestra starting deep in his brain and travelling through his whole body as he pounded the tower-lined streets.

The further he walked, the more the volume increased until it was a roar in his head, blocking out the roar of the traffic and his thoughts, and soon he knew that just walking wasn't going to be enough.

Johnny had only just figured out that the music in his head was the final scene in *Swan Lake* – the one where he or Liam would have to leap – when he realised what he wanted to do.

He cut through a path along the backs of some terraced houses, just like the one he used to live in. The alleyway was narrow, strewn with weeds and rubbish, and it smelled of cat pee. But he was alone.

Dumping his school bag at one end, he began to jog. Then he added in a few small steps, little things that Mrs Cray had shown him. Glass crunched underfoot, and he had to be careful; there wasn't any room to stumble, and this wasn't the place to fall.

Jog, jog, jog, step, step, leap!

The end of the alleyway came too soon, so he turned and danced back again and again, getting more confident, speeding up and leaping gently – once, twice, three times – jumping higher and longer, just like Mrs Cray had shown him.

Maybe it was the streak in his hair, or the fact that there was only a tabby cat to judge him, but gradually he felt different.

Lighter.

Stronger.

Less like a human.

Less like himself.

He still wasn't leaping like Mrs Cray, but he was improving. And he recognised something.

He was happy.

There, with just a cat to witness it, he was as happy as he used to be.

'Oy! What are you doing back here?'

A woman's face appeared from behind some flapping washing.

'Ballet!' he shouted, laughing.

'Well, if you don't go and do it somewhere else, I'll call the police!'

'Ballet's not against the law!' he said.

'No, but truanting is.'

'All right, all right, I'm going.'

He jogged and danced back to his bag.

Johnny had just picked it up and turned to go, when he saw something that stopped him as if he had been tasered.

A man was walking down the alley. He had black hair and he wore jeans and the same trench coat as Johnny's dad. From that distance it could've *been* his dad.

And just for a second he forgot that his dad was dead.

The man stopped by a gate and let himself through.

He heard a child's voice shout from the garden, 'Daddy!'

Johnny turned and ran in the opposite direction as fast as he could.

A stinging pain hit him after a few paces. Maybe it was just a stitch, but it felt more like his stomach bleeding liquid fury.

Despite that, Johnny carried on running, his feet beating out his anger.

Thump thump. Not fair.

Thump thump. Not fair.

Thump thump. Not fair.

Thump thump. Not fair.

Thump thump. Not fair.

Not fair.

Nothing was fair any more.

As he reached the main road, Johnny knew where he was going.

He changed direction and headed for Regent's Park.

It was still early morning. Probably not even breaktime yet at school. The park felt like another world. Johnny was totally alone.

He walked past London Zoo and stopped on the bridge over the rushing water.

A grille was catching the leaves and rubbish and feathers – so many tiny feathers – on one side of the bridge. It was revolting.

He continued walking towards the lake. He would just see if there were any swans there today. He knew that seeing them would make him feel better. It was the only thing that would.

His view was blocked at first by the reeds around the edge of the lake, which were thickening up for summer.

He sped up and soon he was running towards the open area where the swans had been before.

There was still no sign of any wildlife.

But there were no people either.

And it was a big open space where he could dance and no one could tell him he was trespassing.

Johnny dumped his bag, then ran along, keeping parallel with the lake, and leapt as high and long and as fluidly as he could, interspersing his jumps with small steps from the show. And then something else, something that came from nowhere, that Mrs Cray hadn't show him.

Johnny spun.

With his arms crossed over his chest, he spun until he felt a strange tightening sensation in his shoulder blades.

And then he spun more until, hot and exhausted, he threw himself down by the edge of the lake, his face so close to the water that he could smell it.

The reflection that stared back took him by surprise. It was definitely him. But he looked different somehow. Older. He pushed it away and the image of his face broke into pieces that rippled like jelly.

Then he scooped up handfuls of the water and let it run over his head, trickling down into his eyes and mouth, not even caring.

Standing up, he let the drips run down on to his clothes and his face dried in the breeze, feeling new and wonderful and different.

A quiet call came from the far side of the lake. '*Heorr . . . Heorr . . .*'

There was no mistaking it.

Glowing against the weeping willows that trailed in the water, a white shape was gliding towards him.

With its head and neck like a cobra about to strike, the swan turned to face Johnny.

He breathed out as it stopped in the centre of the lake, then he slowly stood up.

Johnny didn't stop to take off his shoes or check that no one was watching, or even to think; the decision had been made before he even knew the question.

He waded into the water until it reached right up to his neck.

He pushed past the reeds and weeds that tried to stop him, and then Johnny swam towards the swan.

As he approached, he heard the sound again. '*Heorrrr . . . heorrr . . .*'

From the back of his throat Johnny returned the call, and it wasn't like any noise he'd ever made before.

The swan waited, watching him as he swam, and in its gaze Johnny felt whole and warm and right.

Then the swan abruptly turned and sped away from the shore. It moved so fast that it cut through the water, leaving a wake like a boat. Dipping its great neck, it disappeared past ropes hung with a sign.

DANGER – KEEP OUT

'Come back!' Johnny said.

But already he was following, plunging under the ropes himself, and staying down where the world was tinted green so that he could move faster and keep up with the bird's huge leathery feet.

Then the swan slowed down, allowing Johnny to catch up, and he could see that it was heading back to a flock gathered in the distance.

Johnny surfaced to take a breath, then plunged back down, following the dark outlines of its legs and feet moving gently up ahead through the weeds.

One more breath and he would be there. Johnny took a lungful of air, and he caught up.

Gasping, he surfaced and was face to face with the swan.

It waited for a moment, its pedalling feet not even rippling the water, while Johnny's graceless strokes sent waves out all around him, ruffling the smooth, glass surface.

The swan dipped its neck in his direction, as if about to speak, then turned and continued swimming towards the flock.

Johnny smiled. *It's taking me to meet the others*, he thought. And a feeling flooded through him.

Acceptance.

It had waited for him, allowed him to take a breath, and now the swan was leading him back to its flock.

It trusted him.

But did he trust the swan?

For that matter, did he trust himself?

The thought was only a flicker in the back of his head.

He remembered the swan pinning Liam down, then coming to the lift of his tower block to show him the roof – a place he could have some space.

Yes. He did trust it. Of course he did.

Johnny filled his creaking lungs with air and dived under the surface again, following the swan's white blur. Without it, he would have been disorientated in the opaque green of the lake. But Johnny could see exactly where he was going, and soon – though it can't have been seconds, it must have been minutes – he saw more white shapes shining through, like lamps in the fog.

Johnny increased the strength of his strokes. He'd already been underwater longer than he thought possible, but he wasn't going to come up for air until he had arrived properly. Until he was in the centre of the group.

Which was weird. He trusted that one swan – his swan. But the whole group? At school, where he should have felt safe, there was no way he would walk right into the middle of a bunch of kids he didn't know.

But here, past the safety barrier, in a lake no one was supposed to swim in, surrounded by wild creatures, he felt completely sure that it was the right thing to do.

So he continued swimming, his strokes getting stronger with every pull until, at last, just above him, was an expanse of white only broken by pairs of black triangles, paddling like clockwork toys.

Johnny found a gap in the group and now, lungs about to burst, he allowed his body to rise slowly to the surface.

As the water cleared from his eyes, Johnny saw seven white heads looking at him, their beaks – orange and black, like coral snakes – pointing in his direction.

He wanted to smile, to laugh, to say hello, but before he could, a hand seemed to grab his lungs and squeeze. Suddenly he was coughing and spluttering, and his stomach was contracting violently, and then everything went green as he plummeted down, hard and fast, into the cloudy water.

The lake was deep and thick with weeds; their finger-like tendrils stroked then wrapped themselves around him, as he sunk to the bottom among old beer cans and bottles half buried in the silt.

As he bumped against the soft ground, Johnny seemed to wake up and panic. He thrashed around, pulling at the weeds that were binding him.

And then he saw two white shapes appear.

He felt them snatch at his clothes and begin to tow him towards the light, until he was crashing through the surface, gasping.

Coming together, the swans' huge warm bodies formed a platform for Johnny to hold on to while he retched and fought for breath and his head stopped spinning, and when he was breathing normally again, the swans carried him over to the larger island, where Johnny could stagger on to land.

'Thank you,' he rasped.

'*Heorrrr . . . heorrr . . .*' they replied, the sound echoing around the lake.

Something had changed in Johnny's head. It must have done, because he felt a strange calm descend.

He didn't question why the flock would have called him over to them, or saved his life when he faltered.

He knew that the swans had done it because there was something in him they recognised.

And he loved them for it.

As he lay there, the June rays began to dry his clothes. The swans surrounded him so that anyone looking could not have seen the boy in a wet school uniform, his eyes shut against the sun and his lips turned in a smile.

Chapter Eight

Thursday

'Ah, Johnny. Running late?'

They had all overslept. Johnny was exhausted from his swim in the lake, and his mum had had to threaten a bucket of icy water to rouse him. Then they'd had a row because the school had been in touch about him bunking, and she had refused to believe his explanation that it must be a computer error.

So it was already 9:30A.M. when Johnny was running towards school and his path was blocked by the not-inconsiderable bulk of Mrs Cray.

She let out a small, high-pitched sound, then whispered, 'Your hair!'

'Er, yeah, it sort of just happened yesterday.'

She smiled, took a deep breath, then hooked her arm through his. 'Shall we go in together?'

Although he didn't reply, she washed him towards the school like a wave towards shore, chatting all the way, apparently not minding his silence.

At the reception, Mrs Cray said, 'Morning, ladies. Can you sign Johnny in as an authorised late? I'm afraid he was held up doing something for the show.'

The receptionist frowned, but wrote it down and buzzed them both in.

'Right then, you,' Mrs Cray said. 'Follow me.'

'But I'm missing Maths,' Johnny said.

'Maths?' She looked offended. 'This is *dance*!'

She led him to the hall and up on to the stage.

Johnny was surprised how different it felt: more serious somehow. He had never been into acting, so this was his first time on a stage. It smelled strange: of floor polish and dust from the velvet curtains. Everything was louder and Mrs Cray's amplified voice carried around the whole room. He wasn't sure he liked it.

'We've got half an hour before the hall's needed for assembly. So come on, show me what you've got.'

He frowned. 'What do you mean?'

'The leap, Johnny, the leap!' Mrs Cray's eyes, usually so calm, were on fire. 'I presume that you do want to do it after all?'

Johnny looked towards the door, ready to run if she got any crazier.

'Yeah. Yeah, I do,' he said.

She clapped her hands together.

'Good,' she said. 'Because you've started so well. And I want you to be 100% on the technical so that the rest can follow. I want body and soul working together. So let's leap!'

She led him to the corner, and together they ran and jumped. Her leaps were fluid and strong, her body shifting effortlessly into the perfect shape.

Johnny's body was exhausted, he was terrified of falling off the stage and, in comparison, his leaps were weak and lopsided.

But, strangely, Mrs Cray clapped. 'It's an improvement,'

she said. 'Yes, it was a bit scrappy, but something huge has changed.'

Johnny thought about the day before. Something had changed.

Something huge.

'But,' Mrs Cray continued, 'you're still not ready. You're not letting go completely. You need to get into flow, the state where you're so involved in an activity that you don't feel like yourself any more. You escape.'

He thought about Mojo at the table and how he got lost in drawing. Johnny wanted to feel like that, he really did, and he knew that he could do it out by himself in an alleyway or by the side of the lake – but there, with Mrs Cray watching, wasn't working for him.

'Once more?' Mrs Cray asked.

He shook his head. He'd had enough.

'Can I go back to Maths, please?' he said.

She put her head to one side, like she was considering something.

'It will all be all right in the end,' she said. 'It might not be perfect, but it will be all right. So, I'll see you at lunchtime for the rehearsal.'

Johnny had no intention of going into a class late. It was going to be bad enough when people saw his hair without drawing extra attention to himself, so he headed for the nearest toilets.

Although it was lesson time, a small group of emo Year Elevens were in there skiving. They eyed him suspiciously.

Johnny didn't look their way. He just used the toilet, then washed his hands, keeping his head down.

But he could feel them staring at him.

Was he about to be beaten up?

'Nice hair,' one said. 'Really cool. How did you do it?'

Johnny looked up and checked the kid's expression. He wasn't being sarcastic.

'Dunno. It just happened.'

'I like it,' said another.

Johnny stepped out into the corridor, smiling.

But second lesson had just ended, and he hit a wall of bodies.

'Look at Swan Boy! He's turned into a skunk!'

'Skunk Boy!'

Everyone stopped and turned; laughter echoed around the walls.

'What do you think you look like?'

'Ha, ha, ha!'

'Oh, my God, what a weirdo!'

Johnny tried to let it wash over him. He imagined himself in the lake again. He bit his lip and clenched his fists.

Nothing worked.

'Shut up!' he said under his breath. 'What's wrong with you lot?'

He tried to picture the swan, floating, serene. He tried to make himself like the swan. But it didn't have the right effect.

'Yeah, he stinks like a skunk too!'

He turned towards the nearest laughing face and swung his fist.

'Oh, no, you don't!'

A hand on his shoulder pulled him backwards before his knuckles even made contact.

'Right.' A teacher was towering over him. 'You're coming to see the Head.'

Johnny looked up at the ticking clock. He'd been waiting in the head teacher's lobby for half an hour. Still, it was better than being in lessons.

'Enter!'

He shuffled in, hands in his pockets, looking down at his feet.

Mr Price had a file open on his desk.

'Sit down.'

He slammed the file shut, then rubbed his balding head.

'Johnny, you've only been here a short while and this is the second time we've met. And, in addition, I've just seen an unathorised absence from yesterday.' He leaned forward on his elbows. 'I'm very disappointed, and I expect your parents will be too.'

'Mum,' he said. 'It's just my mum.'

Mr Price leaned back again and sighed as if that explained everything.

'What sort of a school do you think this would be if we all went around hurting each other willy-nilly?'

Johnny looked down at the marks on his hands from Liam's shoes.

'Physical assaults will not be tolerated at St George's – whatever the provocation. And as a sanction I was going to put you on litter-pick duty. However, I've been speaking to Mrs Cray and I understand that your presence is required at lunchtimes for the show, so, in this instance, your punishment will be deferred.'

He sucked air over his teeth, as if letting Johnny off litter-picking physically hurt him.

'However, if I have to speak to you again, you will forfeit your lead role in the show for a minor part on the playing fields in a high-vis vest.' He raised his voice. 'Do you understand?'

'Yes, sir,' Johnny muttered.

As he stood up, the head teacher said, 'And, Johnny, do

something about the hair. Outlandish hairstyles aren't really going to help you to fit in here.'

'It's not –'

'Don't answer back, boy. Now leave before I change my mind.'

Word about Johnny's hair had already reached his next class, Geography.

They seemed to be waiting for him to come in and the laughter was even louder than it had been in the corridors.

Johnny ignored it and made his way to the back where Stefan was sitting, and took the chair next to him.

'I heard,' Stefan said, ''bout the hair.'

Johnny sat down. 'Apparently it's hilarious.'

Stefan shrugged. 'It's not so bad. I mean, you're not bald, are you? My old man's as bald as a billiard ball. I'm just like him so I'm enjoying my hair while I've got it.' He smoothed down his greasy fringe.

Johnny laughed.

'Yeah, I s'pose things could be worse.'

'They could always be worse,' Stefan said. 'I've got a sister.'

'What's that got to do with anything?'

'Nothing. I was just saying some people are worse off than you. That's all.'

'What's she like, then, this sister?'

'Like Satan,' Stefan whispered. 'In lipstick and heels.'

Lola came into the room.

'Compared to her, Lola's a kitten,' he said.

Lola glared in their direction.

'*Miaow*,' Stefan said to Johnny, and they both grinned.

That day Johnny and Stefan went to the canteen together. It felt weird having someone to talk to while he ate. But it was familiar too, from back in the days when everything was all right.

Of course, the laughter and pointing and Skunk Boy comments continued, but Johnny could tell that he was becoming old news. Soon there would be someone else to pick on.

It wasn't only that which made him feel more cheerful.

His sore ribs were a reminder that Liam had now had his revenge, and the debt that Johnny had somehow found himself owing had been paid in full.

Maybe he was over the worst of it.

If he dyed his hair black again and made an effort, perhaps he could start to blend in and be like everyone else.

'Come on,' said Stefan. 'Rehearsal time.'

Ballet wouldn't help him to fit in. He knew that.

Johnny looked past Stefan and out of the window, where a few green blobs were already litter-picking.

Maybe he should give up the show.

He was loving the dance, but it wasn't the kind of thing to do if he wanted to blend in.

Across the room he saw Liam and Jonas heading out of the canteen.

That made his mind up. He would do it. If Liam could do ballet and still keep his place as the head of the Year Nine mafia, why should Johnny give it up?

He pushed his chair back and stood up.

'Come on, then, wiz,' he said to Stefan.

'Your majesty,' Stefan replied, bowing.

'Don't be weird,' Johnny replied.

'You started it,' said Stefan.

'Yeah, but . . .'

They both laughed, and headed off to the gym.

★ ★ ★

111

The *Swan Lake* music was playing and everyone was gathered when they arrived.

'Today,' said Mrs Cray, rubbing her hands together, 'we're going to be focusing on the nightclub scene.'

'Did they have nightclubs in the olden days?' asked Stefan. 'I mean, they didn't have sound systems, did they? Or coloured lights?'

Someone tried beatboxing the *Swan Lake* music. '*Bkt Ts-Ts, Bkt Ts-Ts, Bkt-Bkt-Bkt, Ts-Ts.*'

Mrs Cray smiled. 'You know, coming together to dance is universal, and as ancient as our species. Whether it's around a campfire or in a modern nightclub, people have always done it.'

'We all wanna have fun,' added Stefan.

But Mrs Cray frowned. 'Dance can be fun, but it can also be deadly serious. What if I told you that some dances change lives? Change the world, even?'

'Don't see how our dance is going to change anything,' Lola said.

Mrs Cray shrugged. 'You'd be surprised. And then there are the dances that ease the passage from childhood to adulthood, which are some of the oldest and most important in many cultures.'

'It'll take more than a poncey dance to make those two into men.'

Johnny recognised the voice coming from behind him as Liam's. So much for being off his radar. Liam clearly still hated him.

'So,' continued Mrs Cray, ignoring the comment, 'scene two. Setting: a nightclub. Roles: Johnny, you're drunk and unhappy; Stefan, you're encouraging the Prince to get even more drunk so that you can get him into trouble; Lola, you're being employed by Stefan to try

112

and tempt the Prince. The rest of you are partygoers. OK?'

The scene was even less like traditional ballet than anything they had done so far, and some of the moves, where they stuck out their bums and did funny walks, just made them all laugh.

Even Liam looked like he was enjoying himself.

While the others carried on practising, Mrs Cray called Johnny and Phoebe over.

'Immediately before the nightclub you two will have a row.' Mrs Cray turned to Johnny. 'Your mother feels like you've let her down. You beg for her forgiveness, but she casts you out; so, pained and drunk, you head off into the night. Got that?'

They both nodded.

She showed them the steps, but Johnny found it hard to concentrate because he realised that Liam, on the other side of the room, was no longer practising.

He was staring over, his eyebrows down and his top lip curled in disgust.

'And bend your knees here before you jump,' Mrs Cray was saying, as Johnny tried a complicated move. 'Good, that's lovely, but don't forget to breathe.'

She beckoned to Phoebe.

'And now, I'll show you both how to do the lift.'

She took Phoebe by the waist and spun her around.

'Your turn now, Johnny.'

Johnny looked over at Liam, who flattened his hand and drew it across his throat in an *I'm going to kill you* movement.

Johnny didn't understand what was going on. Why would Liam care about him dancing with Phoebe?

'Come on, Johnny. Just grasp her here.' Mrs Cray showed him again. 'She doesn't weigh much.'

113

He paused.

Mrs Cray frowned. 'Stop thinking. Just let your body feel.'

He looked back over at Liam. Phoebe and Mrs Cray followed his gaze, but Liam pretended to be practising a jump.

'Ready?'

Johnny stepped forward and reached out towards Phoebe's waist.

'Shoulders down and long necks, both of you.'

He couldn't help it: Johnny's eyes flicked towards Liam again. Now he was smacking the fist of one hand into the palm of the other and smiling.

What should Johnny do?

Run out?

Refuse to do the move?

Pretend to faint?

The possibilities were limited.

But with Mrs Cray waiting, and now the whole class, who seemed to sense that something was up, watching too, he knew that there was only one choice.

An honourable death.

Johnny placed his hands around Phoebe's waist and picked her up. She wasn't much heavier than Mojo and, as he swung, her pale hair spun out around her head as if she were on a fairground ride.

The door banged shut as Liam Clark left the room.

'See?' said Mrs Cray. 'Easy.'

'Yeah, easy,' Johnny repeated, as the gym door continued to swing from the force of Liam's exit.

As soon as Mrs Cray went over to see the other dancers, Johnny found Stefan.

'Wasn't Liam going out with Lola?' he asked.

Stefan shook his head. 'Keep up. He finished with her

yesterday. Apparently he asked Phoebe out. He didn't look very happy with you, did he?'

Just when he thought Liam Clark might leave him alone, it looked like Johnny had handed him another reason to hate him.

'I can't win,' he said.

'Then don't bother trying,' said Stefan. 'I don't.'

'Yeah, and you pay him for the pleasure of not beating you up.'

Stefan looked hurt. 'Used to,' he said. 'I've decided I'm not giving Liam any more money. Actually, I was inspired by you.'

'Eh?'

'Yeah, you survived a beating from Liam, so I will too. Besides, my dad's really suspicious and he'd go mad if he found out I was getting bullied. So I've decided to stop.'

Johnny laughed. 'It's not like that. You can't just decide to stop getting bullied.'

Stefan shrugged. 'Maybe you can. Maybe it's a state of mind. Anyway, we'll see, won't we?'

Chapter Nine

Johnny reached Mojo's school by 3:11p.m. He got there in under ten minutes and hardly broke a sweat. He wondered how he'd managed it – a week before he'd been out of breath after just walking up the stairs.

Mojo was full of energy so the two brothers jogged home together, holding hands. It wasn't very comfortable for Johnny, but at least he knew that Mojo was safe.

Back at the flat Johnny relaxed in front of the TV and let Mojo draw until their mum came home.

As soon as she stepped inside, Mojo flew at her and started talking about the reading cards he had brought home from school.

'I can nearly read them all!' he said. 'And I'm allowed to keep them for ever!'

His mum smiled and hugged him.

'Well done! You'd better show me.'

She had tested Mojo on the first few cards when Johnny came through to the living room. 'What's for dinner, Mum?'

'OK, I suppose I should get on with cooking. Can you take over here though?'

Johnny lifted the top card from the little pile and held it up.

'House,' Mojo said.

He held up the next one.

'Dog.' Mojo did a little excited bounce. 'Quick, next one.'

Johnny held it up.

'Brother. Ooh!' Mojo took it from him, put a piece of tape on the back and stuck the card to Johnny's sweatshirt. 'My teacher said we should stick the words on things so we can learn to spell them.'

'Great, so I have to wear this until you know it?'

Mojo nodded.

'OK. B-r-o-t-h-e-r,' Johnny spelled it out. 'Now shut your eyes and you say it.'

'No, you don't say "bee",' said Mojo. 'You say "buh".'

Johnny took the label off and stuck it on to Mojo's T-shirt.

Mojo smiled. 'Oh, yeah! I'm a brother too. B-r-o– It's loooong.'

'Get me a card and I'll make you one that says "idiot" if you like. That's shorter.'

'Johnny!' Typical of his mum to hear that.

'Sorry, Mum. Only joking.'

She came over and smiled down at Mojo with his stack of cards.

'Isn't he doing well? He could be reading fluently soon if he starts to concentrate a bit more in class.'

'Hey, I can do that too, y'know,' Johnny said, grabbing a card from the very bottom of the pile. 'D-a-d.'

Mojo looked around the room as if he had lost something, then his face dropped. He snatched the card from

Johnny and walked into the kitchen. There was the sound of ripping, then the lid of the bin swinging shut.

His mum shook her head.

'Sorry,' Johnny mouthed. He didn't seem to be able to do anything right any more.

'So,' said his mum, changing the subject, 'did anyone mention your hair today?'

Johnny shrugged. 'No, not really.'

What was the point in her knowing? It wasn't like his mum could do anything about it.

She nudged him. 'See! I told you. You didn't trust me, but I was right. You kids nowadays are all about diversity. It's cool to be different.'

'Yeah,' he said, laughing to himself.

'Anyway, I'm glad, especially because I forgot to buy the dye. I'm really sorry, Johnny.'

'It doesn't matter.'

'Also, I know I'm not winning any mum awards this evening, but do you mind if I pop out after dinner? I'm meeting up with some friends from work. I won't be late – I'll be back by ten.'

'Friends?'

'Yes,' she said.

'But you never used to go out with friends.'

She sighed. 'You know what, Johnny? I've decided it's time I should.'

When they had finished eating, his mum got changed into some clothes that Johnny had never seen before. Then she put on her work coat, the shiny black one that matched her hair. She used to be blonde. But she'd dyed her hair dark when they moved. She'd said she wanted a fresh start and a new look.

119

For Johnny, it made the distance seem even greater between now and then.

'I shouldn't be late. But please make sure Mojo's in bed by seven thirty. He's exhausted.'

'Did you hear that, Mojo?' Johnny called in his direction.

Mojo barked three times, then continued staring blankly at the television.

'Is he a dog again?' Johnny asked.

She nodded. ''Fraid so. And I was just getting used to the tiger.' She paused before opening the door. 'We could see the doctor about the streak. If you want.'

Johnny ran his fingers through the front of his hair. 'No,' he said. 'I'm kind of getting used to it.'

She put on a fake cheerful smile. 'Good. It suits you.' Then she stepped forward and pinched his cheek. 'See you later, handsome.'

'Get off,' he said, though he liked it really.

As soon as the front door clicked shut, Mojo got his pens, then pulled back the tablecloth.

Johnny sat with him while he drew.

The table was now half filled with his pictures. They were running around the edge and moving in towards the middle, like water going down a plughole.

'What are you going to draw tonight?' Johnny asked.

Mojo didn't answer for a moment, then said in his mum's voice, 'Haven't you got homework to do?'

Johnny laughed. 'Probably.'

He didn't want to be told what to do by a five-year-old, but he emptied his school bag anyway, and found the feather at the bottom. It was a bit grubby, so he took it into the bathroom and ran it under the tap, then dried it carefully with a piece of toilet roll.

Next he smoothed the feather down, combing it with his fingers until the barbs zipped together neatly. Holding it up to the light, he caught sight of his hair in the mirror.

He took off his school shirt and positioned the feather stretching out over his shoulder, making a tiny wing.

If only he had a few more . . .

'Johnny! I need a wee!'

Johnny jumped guiltily, then put the feather in his pocket and pulled his shirt back on.

He let Mojo in.

'You shouldn't wait 'til you're desperate.' Now *he* was sounding like his mum.

Mojo dropped his trousers and, holding one leg up to the side, aimed a stream at the toilet bowl.

It missed.

'Mojo, you can't cock your leg!' Johnny shouted.

Mojo growled at him, then waddled out with his trousers still round his ankles.

Johnny sighed. He didn't want to leave it for his mum, so he mopped up the pee, dripping it all over himself in the process. Great, now everyone would think he had wet himself.

Back in the kitchen, he picked up a Maths sheet that had been at the bottom of his bag.

He hadn't done much homework recently, but it was linear equations and he already knew how to do them.

He got a pen out of his pencil case and held it over the first one, but his mind went blank just before it touched the paper.

He sighed and put the pen back, then he screwed up the sheet and threw it in the bin.

Then he got it out again and put it in the recycling.

Mojo was still drawing.

'Hey, d'you want to watch some TV?' Johnny asked.

Mojo didn't reply, so Johnny sat through a couple of American comedies, even though he'd seen them before. Finally they finished, and a programme about house-hunting came on, with a couple from Ealing who were 'desperate to leave the urban jungle behind them'.

As they snooped around bungalows in Wales, Johnny wandered over to the window and looked down.

It didn't look like a jungle to him. It looked ordered and beautiful. Especially at night from above, with the city lights glinting. It was like Christmas all year long.

He didn't understand why anyone would want to live surrounded by muddy fields and sheep. He'd been to the countryside once. It stank.

Johnny followed a bus travelling along Fellows Road. From all the way up there Johnny could see that bus roofs were white. He hadn't known that until he had moved into the flat.

The bus stopped just by the kebab shop.

'I love kebabs,' he said to himself. Then he breathed on the pane, drew a heart in the mist and wrote *JE* for *Johnny Emin* at the top and *KB* underneath.

His dad had been half Turkish, and he used to take Johnny to the restaurants in Dalston for a doner. Although he couldn't speak the language very well, Johnny remembered him reading out the menus, pronouncing all the dishes properly.

'Der-ner ki-ybap. Ishkem-bay chor-baser. I-mam buy-elder'.

Johnny looked over at Mojo. As his older brother, he had to be the one to take him for his first kebab. His dad never would.

Maybe tonight would be a good opportunity.

He looked at the clock on the mantelpiece. 6:40P.M. Johnny was starving. The dinner his mum had made had hardly touched the sides. He most definitely had room for a doner.

'Mojo, d'you fancy going for a little walk?'

Mojo didn't raise his head. 'We're not allowed to go out.'

'Oh, come on. We wouldn't be long.'

Mojo looked up then, frowning. 'No, it's late. I don't want to go outside when it's late. It's dangerous.'

'But it's not even dark yet. And going out anytime isn't dangerous for dogs. They can see really well in the dark – which it's not,' he added.

Mojo carried on drawing.

Johnny sighed. 'OK, forget it.'

He rubbed out the condensation heart with his sleeve, then turned back to the couple on the TV who weren't sure they could put up with a phone mast near their dream home.

But he couldn't stop thinking about kebabs.

Steaming hot, succulent meat with crunchy lettuce.

He looked over at Mojo again and watched him yawn. It was all right for him. He wasn't hungry. His stomach was probably half the size of Johnny's.

Kebabs. Kebabs. Kebabs.

Johnny realised that he hadn't been out at night for ages.

He had an idea.

Johnny crept over to the clock and, after fiddling with the back for a minute, managed to turn the hands so that it said 7:25P.M.

'Nearly bedtime, Mojo.'

'Really?' He looked at the clock.

Johnny felt briefly guilty at tricking him into an early bedtime, but he pushed the feelings aside.

Kebabs. Kebabs. Kebabs.

It wasn't like it would make much difference to Mojo. Anyway, he figured, sleep is good for you.

Mojo put the caps on his pens and pulled the tablecloth back over to hide the drawings.

'OK,' Johnny said. 'Brush your teeth and straight into bed.'

He waited until Mojo had finished, then stood at the doorway ready to turn out the light.

'What about a story?'

Johnny's stomach rumbled. 'You're too big for stories.'

Mojo's mouth drooped and Johnny thought he was going to howl.

'OK, OK. Wait a minute.' He went to his cupboard and took out an old superhero comic. 'You can read this. It's mostly drawings anyway.'

Mojo looked suspicious, but took it from him.

Johnny left him turning the pages and went back into the living room.

After a few minutes of a cookery programme where they shot pigeons and made them into a huge pie to feed a village, he crept back into the bedroom. The comic was lying on Mojo's chest. His eyes were shut and he was breathing deeply.

Johnny gently slid open the drawer where he kept his birthday money.

'What are you doing, Johnny?'

Johnny bit his lip. 'Nothing,' he said. 'Go to sleep.'

He got back to the TV in time to see the pie go into an enormous oven, and watched a team of chefs whisking eggs and sugar for a giant meringue.

It had been ages. Mojo had to be asleep by now. Johnny crept to the door and listened.

Rustling paper. *Seriously?*

Why had he given him such an interesting comic? It wasn't going to work.

The vision of kebabs faded.

Johnny would have to go out another time.

The meringue on the TV was in the oven now. He went to the window and opened it a crack so that he could smell the sharp fresh air.

He didn't usually mind looking after Mojo, but most kids of his age were hanging out with their friends or at football training. If nothing had changed, if his dad hadn't died and they were still living in Timbuktu Road, that's what he would have been doing, and his mum would have been there looking after Mojo, instead of the other way round.

None of this was his fault, so he should have nothing to feel guilty about.

Not really.

Kebabs. Kebabs. Kebabs.

Johnny heard a loud snore from the bedroom.

He tiptoed to the doorway.

'Mojo, you awake?' he whispered.

Another snore.

'Mojo.' He said it louder.

Silence.

He crossed the room and poked Mojo in the back.

No response.

'Mojo, d'you want a sweetie?' he whispered.

Nothing.

'Or a doggy treat?'

Mojo snuffled, then settled back down.

Johnny punched the air. Then he took some of his birthday money from the open drawer and put it in his pocket.

He crept out and locked the front door, bounced down the stairs two at a time, and in seconds he was standing in the evening air.

It felt so great to be out of the flat that Johnny had to stop himself from dancing.

Instead he speed-walked along Fellows Road. Quite a few shops were still open, and he joined the stream of people making their way home.

The kebab shop seemed a bit further away than he had thought, but after about five minutes he spotted the red sign with yellow lettering boasting, *The Best Kebab House*.

Kebabs. Kebabs. Kebabs.

Kebabs!

He ran the last few steps and, as he pushed through the door, he was met with a familiar warm meaty smell.

Mmmm . . . It was like he was inhaling a doner.

Johnny ate on the way back. The first bite had been delicious, but halfway through he started to feel sick, and he dumped it in a bin and ran home.

He let himself into the flat. Everything was as he had left it.

Then he heard a small voice. 'You went out. And I'm telling Mum.'

Mojo was standing in front of him, his hair stuck down on one side.

'I'm sorry, Moj. It was just for a moment.'

Mojo stared, unblinking.

'Were you chasing another feather?'

'Yeah, sort of.'

126

'I was scared,' Mojo said. 'I thought you weren't going to come back. Like Dad.'

Johnny stepped forward and hugged him. 'I'm sorry.'

'Do you think Dad's going to come back soon though?'

'I . . .' Johnny had been going to say he didn't know. *I shouldn't have to deal with this*, he thought. *It should be my mum having these conversations.*

But someone had to start telling Mojo the truth.

Not that they hadn't tried many times.

He took a deep breath. 'No, Mojo, Dad can't come back.'

'But he might,' Mojo said.

'No, he won't. Because he can't.'

Mojo's face brightened. 'Did you find it?'

'Find what?'

'The feather?'

'Er . . . Yeah,' Johnny lied.

'Can I have it?'

'Course. You go to sleep now and I'll give it to you in the morning.'

'OK. You'd better though. Or I'm telling. And I'm not even joking.'

As he got into bed and turned over, Mojo muttered, 'And Mum would kill you.'

'You're not wrong,' said Johnny.

He reached under his bed. The feather was lying, wrapped in tissue, next to the letter about the paperweight and a leaflet that his old school counsellor had given him.

Johnny pushed the letter further back and brought out the feather and the leaflet.

He stared at the cover: a sunrise, or maybe a sunset. At the top it said: *Saying goodbye.*

127

He knew what was inside. It was divided into sections, explaining the different stages people go through when they lose someone they love.

Stage One was denial – not believing that the person has really gone.

Stage Two was anger.

He hadn't read any more of it. It made him too angry. His dad was gone – how was this going to help?

Johnny stashed the leaflet underneath the bed again and carefully tucked the feather inside his pillowcase.

That night he dreamt of being back on the lake with the swans. He could swim really fast and dive under for ages without getting out of breath.

But then he saw Mojo and his mum on the shore.

Mojo was shouting, 'Swan Boy! Look, it's the Swan Boy.'

And Johnny tried to call back, 'It's just me, Mojo. It's Johnny!'

But they didn't recognise him.

Chapter Ten

Friday

When Johnny woke early the next morning, he could hear Mojo barking.

He took the feather from his pillowcase and stumbled into the kitchen.

'Here you go,' he said, and put it down next to Mojo's bowl.

His mum stopped with her spoon halfway to her mouth.

'Get that dirty thing away from his food!'

Mojo looked at her and growled.

'And I've already told you: no doggy stuff at the table.'

Mojo bared his teeth, picked up his bowl of cereal and took it to the corner of the kitchen. He put it on the floor and lapped like a dog, getting milk in his hair and slopping puffed rice all over the place.

'Did you let him stay up late?' said his mum. 'I bet you did. It always makes him grumpy.'

Johnny relaxed. So Mojo hadn't told her. He supposed that was one advantage of Mojo communicating in barks and yelps. But still, he was impressed. Not many five-year-olds could keep a secret like that.

'Yeah, sorry,' he said. 'It's just, we were having a good time.'

Mojo looked up, his face bearded with milk. He narrowed his eyes.

'Walkies,' he snarled.

'Don't be silly,' snapped Mum. 'It's a school day.'

'Maybe I'll take you to the park tomorrow,' Johnny said. 'You can run around with the local pit bulls.'

Mojo barked, then tried to scratch himself with his back leg, unbalanced and fell into his bowl.

'Oh, Mojo!' his mum shouted. 'Now you'll have to get changed. Go and get a clean pair of trousers.'

Mojo didn't move, just started a low, menacing growl.

'I mean it,' said his mum. 'Go and get changed.'

Mojo's growl got louder and Johnny knew he was getting to the point of no return.

'I'll get them,' Johnny said, leaving the table and going to the wardrobe they shared.

He ran back with the clean clothes, and Mojo was still on the floor, but now he was crouched and about to attack.

His mum was ignoring it, which was what the psychologist had said to do – praise the good behaviour, ignore the bad – but Johnny could see that she was worried.

'Come on, Mojo,' he said, crouching down next to him. 'I'll help you put these on.'

His mum looked up at the clock that Johnny had changed the night before and shrieked. 'Nine o'clock! It can't be! Come on, you two, we're nearly an hour late!'

'No, the clock's wrong,' Johnny said.

But Mum didn't hear because at that moment Mojo pounced and latched his jaws on to Johnny's wrist.

130

'Ow! Get off! That hurts!'

His mum ran over and pulled Mojo off, and he sank his teeth into her arm this time, breaking the skin, before running into the bedroom.

'You OK?' Johnny asked his mum.

'Yes, I think so,' she said, but her face was flushed. 'What about you?'

Johnny rubbed the little red indents on his arm. 'I'll live.'

He saw a tear roll down her cheek.

'Cheer up,' Johnny said. 'At least he hasn't got rabies.'

His mum didn't smile.

'It's nothing to joke about.' Then she said in a low voice, 'You know, it's at times like this that I really miss your dad.'

There was no way that Johnny wanted to get involved in another conversation about his dad, so he pretended he hadn't heard, picked up the forgotten feather from the table and went into the bedroom.

Mojo was lying face down. When he heard Johnny come in, he turned towards the wall, leaving a little dark patch on the pillow where his tears had soaked in.

'Here,' Johnny said. 'Why don't you take this to school? It might help you to have a good day.'

He put the feather on the pillow next to Mojo's face and crept out.

Johnny counted the comments at school that day.

Skunk Boy: 4
Badger: 1
Grandad: 1
Weirdo: 2
Swan Boy: 6

Only fourteen insults in six hours. He was pleased. Things were definitely getting back to normal. Soon, if things continued, he would be the kid that people despised quietly. He hoped so anyway.

There was another after-school rehearsal later. His mum had arranged to leave work early so she could pick up Mojo.

The day whizzed by and Johnny was soon standing in front of Mrs Cray as she tucked her long hair behind her ears and clapped her hands to get their attention.

'My wonderful fellow artists, I can't tell you how delighted I am that you're all here again, and ready to put your hearts, minds and bodies into this production.'

Her gaze swept across the room, taking them all in. 'Together we can silence our critics and make this the best show the school has ever seen. In fact, I'm so convinced that it's going to be a resounding success that I've invited the local paper to come along and write a review.'

'A review? What, with our names in and everything?' Stefan asked.

'Yes.'

'That would be cool,' Stefan said.

'Yeah, but what if we're rubbish?' Liam asked.

Mrs Cray raised an eyebrow. 'Let's not allow that to happen.'

No one wanted to look like an idiot in print, so they threw themselves into the rehearsal, working on some of the group dances.

Johnny took a moment to gaze around him, and was shocked by the improvement in them all.

With Mrs Cray shouting out the beat – 'And, one–two–three, one–two–three' – they got through the scenes, jumping, stamping, marching and bending roughly in time with each other. Soon they were all red-faced and grunting, and stinking of BO.

It still wasn't pretty, but it was better.

Mrs Cray, however, wasn't satisfied.

'Higher!', 'Lower!' and 'With the music!' she shouted until her voice was croaky.

Finally most of them were allowed to sit down while she taught Stefan and Phoebe their 'pas de deux', as she called it.

Stefan was surprisingly good, and seemed to learn his steps quickly.

But it wasn't Stefan that Johnny was staring at.

It was Phoebe. There was something about her. It didn't take him long to realise what it was.

She moved like she was in water.

Like a swan.

'Bravo!' shouted Mrs Cray, with what looked like tears in her eyes.

'Yeah, bravo!' shouted Liam, walking over and grabbing Phoebe's arm – and jabbing Stefan at the same time, without Mrs Cray seeing.

'Don't do that,' Phoebe said.

Johnny wasn't sure he had heard correctly, but the look on Phoebe's face was unmistakable. And so was the look on Liam's.

'C'mon, babe,' he said. 'Stand with us.'

Phoebe shrugged him off and stayed where she was, right next to Stefan.

Johnny resisted the urge to cheer.

Then it was his turn to learn a dance with Lola.

'Now, remember, Johnny,' Mrs Cray said. 'This is the girlfriend who has been chosen for you. But you don't love her. Your heart lies elsewhere. And, one–two–three . . .'

Too right, I don't love her, Johnny thought. He still had the bruises from the attack she'd been part of.

Lola was a good dancer though, and Johnny managed to remember the steps, only standing on her foot once.

But Mrs Cray still wasn't happy. 'Lola, you're supposed to be trying to flirt with him, but it looks more like you want to kill him.'

Lola grinned and shrugged, then turned, grabbed Johnny and kissed him on the lips. As she pulled away she looked over at Liam.

Mrs Cray clapped her hands.

'That's better. But next time, Johnny, step away from her.'

'If I'd seen it coming, I would have,' he said, getting a laugh from the cast and a glare from Lola and Liam.

Mrs Cray smiled. 'Well done, everyone. See you all next week. And keep practising!'

People started moving towards the door, and Johnny was about to leave too, when she stopped him.

'So, Johnny, how's the great leap going?'

'Good.' He tried to sound confident.

'Fantastic. So, come on, let's see where you're at.'

'What, right now?'

A few of the other kids were still hanging around and he really didn't want them to see him make a fool of himself again.

She smiled. 'Yes, now. Don't worry, I don't expect perfection.' She paused. 'Yet.'

Johnny had a familiar sick feeling in his stomach. But saying no to Mrs Cray was almost impossible, so he jogged into the far corner of the gym.

With his back pressed into the two walls, he took a deep breath and tried to picture how she had done it.

The precision of her leading leg as it stretched out in front.

The angle of her back leg as it gently bent behind.

How it didn't look like a jump, more like an effortless stretch that just happened to lift her off the ground and carry her wide across the room.

Like the leap was doing it, not the person.

And how being off the ground was her natural place.

'When you're ready,' Mrs Cray said.

One, two, three, four, five steps and Johnny's legs propelled him.

Up and away.

High and wide, almost like Mrs Cray.

His best ever leap.

And then his feet were back on the floor.

He stumbled a bit, righted himself and waited for Mrs Cray to say how great it was.

She pursed her lips. 'Hmm. Better. It's stronger, more masculine even.' She paused. 'But not good enough.'

He felt anger flare inside him.

'Why? What's wrong with it?'

She narrowed her eyes and it looked like she was watching an action replay in her head.

'As I said, it's better. Technically, that is. It's nearly big enough, and it's the correct shape, though you need to do something about your arms.'

She took a deep breath and frowned.

'But emotionally you don't mean it yet. You haven't learnt to be brave enough. This leap needs a lot of courage. You have to express confidence, freedom, triumph. At the moment you're pretending.' She smiled at him. 'You have it in you to do it, I'm certain of that. Find it inside yourself.' She touched his chest lightly. 'In here.'

She caught his gaze and held it. 'This isn't about the position of your arms and legs, Johnny. It's about the aspect of your heart.'

Johnny just stared at her. He was used to Mrs Cray being a bit odd, but this was another level. Who was she to tell him to be brave? She was just some crazy old teacher at a terrible secondary school.

Confidence? Freedom? Triumph?

He wasn't a ballet dancer. How could he possibly be confident doing something so difficult?

And freedom – he was a kid. Kids don't have freedom. If he did, he certainly wouldn't have been spending his time being criticised by someone like her.

As for triumph, he shook his head as he thought about it. That word wasn't even in his dictionary.

'Now run along,' she said. 'You don't want to be late for your next lesson.'

Johnny walked out of the gym and straight into Liam Clark and his mates leaving the changing room.

'Careful, Swan Boy,' Liam said. 'You don't want to rip your tutu.'

Johnny ignored him and pushed the swinging door to the changing room.

He thought there was no one in there at first.

Then he heard the shower.

The sound of running water stopped and Stefan's voice called out, 'Who's that?'

'It's me. It's Johnny.'

'Johnny, thank God. Pass me my towel and clothes, would you?'

He looked around. There was nothing on the benches. Then he saw them, in a toilet full of yellow water and gently bobbing turds.

'Hurry up!'

'Sorry, Stefan, they're a bit, er . . . wet.'

'Wet? Oh, I don't care. Pass them to me anyway.'

'No, trust me, they're not wearable. Hold on, I'll get something else for you to put on.'

Johnny went to the big black bin that held all the abandoned shorts, odd boots and stinking tracksuit tops, and pulled out a few things that he thought Stefan might be able to fit into.

Then he took a stack of rough green paper towels from a dispenser.

'Here.' He passed them under the cubicle door. 'Sorry, it's the best I could do.'

Johnny waited, listening to Stefan sandpaper himself dry, before he handed over the shiny blue shorts and grey, formerly white, T-shirt.

'You are joking!' Stefan said. 'These are tiny. I can hardly get 'em on!'

'Best I could do, I'm afraid. Unless you wanted a pink swimming costume or a hockey skirt.'

'Might fit better,' he said, opening the door.

The shorts weren't too bad, but the T-shirt stopped above the waistband, leaving a wide belt of Stefan's scarred stomach showing. He folded his arms, trying to hide it.

Johnny didn't want to look, but it was too late. And once he'd seen it there was no point in pretending he hadn't.

'Don't worry,' Stefan said, 'it's not contagious.'

'How did you do it?' Johnny asked.

Stefan rubbed the mass of red lines that licked up his stomach like flames. 'It's just stretch marks,' he said. 'I wasn't fat when I was little. But then my belly grew too fast for my skin to keep up.'

'Isn't there a cure?'

He shrugged. 'I dunno. I'm used to it. It's me now. I'm not ashamed.'

'No, I didn't mean . . .'

'So where's my stuff?'

Johnny pushed open the toilet door.

'Oh.' Stefan sighed.

'Is this cos you haven't paid Liam?'

Stefan smiled. 'Yeah, probably. But maybe it means I won't get beaten up after all? Happy days.'

Johnny laughed. 'Not many people would look so pleased to find their clothes down the toilet.'

'Yeah, well, you've gotta get your happiness where you can. Come on then, pass me that hockey stick.'

They used it to fish Stefan's clothes out of the toilet, then drained them using a tennis racket and put them in a plastic bag.

'I'll have to tell my dad I spilt something. He'd go nuts if he knew.'

'What, he'd come and have a go at Liam?'

Stefan shrugged. 'No, he'd be annoyed with me. For not sticking up for myself, like my sister does.'

'Yeah, but it's not your fault,' Johnny said.

Then he remembered how he used to see people like Stefan when he was at his old school. He thought it was their fault that they were bullied.

As the pair left school together, Liam and some of the Populars were hanging around outside. They must have been waiting to see what Stefan would be wearing.

'Nice outfit, Stephanie!' Jonas shouted.

Liam's mates laughed loudly and wolf-whistled.

Johnny wanted to shout at them, to tell them to leave Stefan alone.

But his ribs still hurt from Liam's attack, and he really didn't want any more trouble with the Populars.

'Oh no, I've just realised I was supposed to pick up my brother,' Johnny lied. 'See you tomorrow.'

He ran past Stefan, who was covering his stretch-marked stomach with his dripping bag.

Before Johnny turned the corner, he looked back. The group was walking towards Stefan and yelling insults.

Johnny thought he heard Stefan shout his name, but he carried on anyway.

The *Swan Lake* music wasn't in his head as he jogged home that day. Instead he thought about what Mrs Cray had said to him about bravery.

She was right. He was a coward.

Back at Burnham Tower, Johnny's mum was cooking and Mojo was staring at the TV.

Johnny sat on the sofa and tried to watch the cartoons with him, but he couldn't concentrate; the guilt wouldn't leave him alone.

Besides, his whole body was tingling with adrenalin. He looked around the living room. It was only about three square metres.

He needed to move.

He needed space to fly.

'There's no room to do anything in this flat,' he moaned.

His mum came in from the kitchen.

'What's wrong?'

Johnny couldn't tell her that he had just left the only person he could possibly call a friend to be beaten up by the school bullies. He couldn't let her hate him as much as he hated himself.

So instead he sat up and said, 'I wish we were still in our old house. At least we had a garden.'

His mum sat down next to him and put her arm around his shoulder. 'I know. I miss the old house too.'

'D'you think anyone else has moved into it?'

'I don't know. Probably.'

Johnny thought. 'Do you think someone dying there would put them off?'

His mum rubbed his arm gently and didn't speak for a moment. 'It's an old house,' she said. 'I'm sure a lot of people have died there. And he didn't die inside. He was out on the street when . . .' Her voice trailed off.

'Even if he had, it wouldn't put me off,' said Johnny.

'Well, some people are superstitious,' she said. 'They believe all sorts of nonsense when it suits them.'

'Like stuff about patron saints?'

She shrugged. 'That's religion. It's different.'

'Don't you believe anything weird?' he said. 'I mean, haven't you ever had, I dunno, lucky socks or something?'

She thought. 'I had a rabbit's-foot key ring once.'

He screwed up his face. 'Eugh.'

'Yeah, I know. It was a bit gross. But it was supposed to be lucky. Not lucky for the rabbit of course.'

'So, did it work?'

'Well, I had my car keys on it and I never had a crash. Then the rabbit's foot fell off.'

'Did you have a crash after you lost it?'

She smiled. 'No. But that's because I'm such a great driver.'

Johnny laughed. His dad always used to tease her about her driving, but he knew that really she was better than him.

And now they didn't even have a car any more.

'If no one else has moved into it, can't we go back to our house? Please? I hate it here.'

She sighed. 'No. I can't afford the rent, not on my wages. And it's too far from my new job.'

'What if I get a job too?'

'Doing what? You're getting too big to fit up a chimney.'

Johnny frowned. 'I'm serious. I could get a job in a shop or a paper round or something.'

'No, love, you just concentrate on your studies.'

He snorted. 'If you'd wanted me to do well you shouldn't have sent me to that school. It's a dump.'

His mum winced, and Johnny knew he'd overdone it. 'Sorry.'

She sighed again. 'Just do your best, love. That's all I ask.'

Johnny stretched his legs out. The urge to move was getting unbearable. It was like having ants in his muscles.

'I just need to go downstairs,' he said. 'I think there was some mail for us.'

She looked surprised. 'Was there? It's very late for the post.'

He nodded.

Making a gesture felt less like a lie than speaking.

'All right, but don't hang around. That front door doesn't lock any more and you never know who might be lurking.'

Johnny ran down to their mailbox. He knew there would be no letters, but he checked it because he had said he would.

Then he went to the lift. Someone had taped the *DANGER – OUT OF ORDER* sign back on to the door, but he could see from the illuminated panel that it was working.

He pressed the button and the door opened.

He stepped inside.

There was no swan in there that day, and, though he hadn't thought there would be, Johnny was a bit disappointed. It meant there was more room, but he still stood with his back against the cold metal wall while the lift jerked its way up.

It reached level eighteen with a cheerful *ding*.

Johnny stood on the threshold, holding the doors open.

There was a moment of indecision, then his legs decided for him, and he stepped on to the surface of the roof.

It was about the same size as the school gym. Apart from some storage boxes and air vents, it was clear. It would be the perfect place to practise his dance. No one would see him and he could come up whenever he wanted.

Johnny still didn't like how high it was. But he'd managed to run right across the roof the last time, so he was sure he'd be able to dance.

He felt so confident as he stepped forward that his legs buckling took him completely by surprise.

He pulled himself up and went back into the lift. Then he tried to walk again, and this time he took one step on to the roof before the trembling and prickles of sweat started, and he fell on to the rough surface like a puppet with its strings cut.

Then he lay back for a few minutes, listening to the buzz from the city below and the beat of his heart.

Above him a flock of birds called and it sounded like they were mocking him for being stuck there. He watched them until they were out of sight.

He had to try again.

He stood up, watching his legs the whole time so he didn't have to look at the horizon, and he thought of the swans at the park. How they waddled, faster and faster, until their feet were a blur, then they took off.

He began to copy them, with small steps – not elegant, that wasn't the point; just getting up some speed – as he jogged, then ran, then sprinted towards the edge, towards the sky.

Then finally his feet were ready to leave the crunchy surface of the roof, ready to soar upwards just like Mrs Cray, just like the swan.

His body grew stronger, lighter, and he stretched forward. He felt his shoulders tingle as his feet finally left the ground.

'Ouf!'

The barrier crashing into his chest knocked the wind out of him.

He opened his eyes and looked down.

He felt sick.

He had nearly run off the roof.

He tried to stay calm. He told himself that the barrier was too high, that he couldn't really have run over it.

Johnny walked back slowly to the lift, and as he stepped in, out of the corner of his eye, he saw a white shape fly off.

His mum was standing by the door when he got back to the flat.

'Johnny, where have you been? How could it possibly take half an hour to check the mail?'

'Sorry.'

'I've got to nip out for some milk. Look after your brother, will you?'

143

Mojo was sitting in his usual place at the table, and as soon as he heard the front door close he got out his pens and started drawing.

Johnny tried to look over his shoulder, but Mojo curled his arm around so that he couldn't see.

Then he looked up. 'You smell, Johnny.'

He sniffed his armpit. Mojo was right, so he went to run himself a bath.

His chest was already sore from where Liam's gang had kicked him, and the encounter with the barrier had made it even worse, so, standing in the dim bathroom light, he stripped off his school jumper, then undid the buttons on his thin shirt to have a look.

But there was no red mark or bruise.

His chest was a shimmering white.

He thought it must be an illusion, maybe a reflection, the light bouncing off the tiles, so he positioned himself directly underneath the bulb and took a closer look.

What on earth?

All across his chest were what looked like wispy white hairs. And in between the hairs were little bumps where more hairs were pushing through.

But that's not possible.

He clutched a towel to his chest, then ran out of the bathroom and past Mojo into the kitchen. He ransacked the drawers, dumping cut-out recipes, discount coupons and bin bags on to the side, before finding it: a mini, plastic magnifying glass that had come in a cracker.

He ran back to the bathroom. Under the light he peered through the lens.

It was un-

believable.

Each little hair had tiny fluffy barbs coming off it.

144

Johnny closed his eyes and breathed in and out deeply to try and get rid of the floaty feeling in his head.

He counted to twenty-five. It seemed like a sensible sort of number.

1234567891011121314151617181920212223242 5.

Then he opened his eyes and looked through the magnifying glass again.

It was undeniable.

He hadn't grown a hairy chest.

He had grown feathers.

Soft, white, downy feathers.

FEATHERS!

Johnny ran his hands lightly over the covering. Then he gave the feathers a gentle tug. 'Ow!'

Three came away, leaving tiny pink holes in his skin.

Like a plucked bird.

His breathing started coming too fast and his head went fuzzy again. He sat on the edge of the bath and tried the eye-shutting thing again, but with the same result.

Feathers.

This was too much. All the strangeness – the storm, the swans and the white streak – was nothing in comparison with feathers. He splashed his face, leaving his eyes open, hoping that he was imagining it.

But when the watery haze cleared, the feathers were still there.

How? I'm human. Humans don't grow feathers.

Johnny climbed into the bath, lowered himself into the warm water and let out a deep breath.

He would have to pull them out. He remembered an Italian boy at his old school who'd had the hairy chest of a fully grown man. A group of Year Elevens had jumped him one lunchtime, held him down and shaved it off.

Imagine what he would be put through if anyone saw that he had the downy chest of a baby bird?

'Johnny!' Mojo banged on the door. 'What are you doing in there?'

Hallucinating, hopefully.

'Nothing,' he said.

'I need you!'

'Just a minute.'

'Hurry, it's important!'

'OK, OK!'

He got out, dried and dressed, then found Mojo on the sofa. 'OK, what's the emergency?'

'I need you to pretend to be Dad.'

Johnny shook his head. 'What, you want me to sit here drinking beer and smoking in front of the TV?'

'No, I want you to give me a piggyback, then I want you to be the tickle monster, then you can draw pictures on my back and I have to guess what they are. And I won't argue at all.'

Johnny sighed. 'Really? Is that what you remember about Dad?'

Mojo nodded. 'And I think he will come back soon. So I want to remember what to do. In case he's forgotten.'

Johnny didn't want to tell him yet again that his dad wasn't coming back.

Instead he said, 'Go on then, climb aboard . . .'

By the time their mum came home, Johnny was exhausted from giving Mojo rides around the room – the pair were giggling and on their fifth round of What's on My Back?

'Sausages and mash for dinner,' she announced.

Johnny groaned. 'Really? Haven't we got any fish fingers or something?'

She frowned. 'You don't like fish, Johnny.'

He frowned back. 'I do now,' he said, though he was surprised too.

Johnny almost forgot about his chest that evening. He watched TV with his mum, which stopped him from having to think, but then it was time for bed – and for the thoughts to run wild.

As he lay there, he wondered if it was his fault that he had grown feathers.

Should he have resisted picking up the first feather, getting into the lift with the swan, swimming in the lake?

Most of all, should he really be trying to learn to fly?

Johnny put his hand inside the T-shirt he wore in bed. The feathers were soft and smooth.

They were amazing. They were unique.

They were his.

But he didn't want to be different.

The feathers would have to go.

Chapter Eleven

Monday

He'd had all weekend to get used to it, but when Johnny woke up to his screaming alarm on Monday morning, the first thing he did was to check underneath his T-shirt.

The down was still there.

Shimmering with health.

He went into the bathroom and stood with his chest bared to the mirror.

His mum's pink razor was resting on the side.

As he had done on both Saturday and Sunday, he wet it under the tap and held it against his skin.

He had to shave the feathers off. There was no way that he could go to school like that. What if someone saw?

His mum knocked on the bathroom door. 'Hurry up, Johnny, you're late!'

He sighed. She was right. He put the razor down and got dressed. He would have to do it later.

'I don't know what you find to do in there,' his mum said as he came out of the bathroom.

'Flossing,' Johnny said, flashing a pearly grin at her.

'But we haven't got any –'

Johnny didn't hear the end of the sentence. He grabbed his bag and, without any breakfast, he ran out of the flat.

Maybe it was adrenalin from the feathers, but once he'd run down the stairs and into the street, his body was itching for more, so he sprinted to school. The exercise from the dance was making him fit, and he felt good.

But as he got closer he slowed down. It wouldn't do to be seen running into school. Running away from school was OK, obviously.

Also, Liam Clark was leaning against the low wall where the Populars gathered.

When he saw Johnny, he pulled out his earphones.

'All right, Swan Boy?' he said.

Johnny nodded, waiting for something else: an insult or a threat.

'Seen your fat girlfriend yet?'

And there it was.

'What d'you mean?'

'Stefan. Or is it Stephanie? She's got some nice eyeshadow on today.'

Liam put the earbuds back in, smiling to himself.

No!

Johnny had been so focused on his feathers that he had forgotten about leaving Stefan at the bus stop.

Forgotten that he had let down his only friend.

Up ahead Johnny saw him. His dark greasy hair was covering his face, and he was walking fast.

'All right, Stefan?' Johnny called out.

He didn't reply.

'What's up?'

Stefan lifted his head and glared at him.

Johnny winced. Stefan's left eye was ringed with a purple bruise.

'That looks painful. It wasn't Liam, was it?'

'What do you think?'

Johnny shrugged. 'Well, I dunno, or I wouldn't be asking, would I?'

There was silence between them for a moment as they walked, then Johnny tried again. 'Is it about the money? Cos if it is, maybe you should pay him. I mean, it's not right, but that looks seriously painful.'

Stefan stopped. 'I did pay him. I gave him my school trip money, but he beat me up anyway. He called it interest.'

Stefan started walking again.

'Wait, you're not blaming me for that, are you?'

Stefan said nothing.

'You must be joking.' Johnny felt guilty, but he was angry too. Stefan had been bullied by Liam long before Johnny started at the school. And it had been his decision to stop paying Liam. No way was this Johnny's fault. 'What, you expected me to protect you?'

Stefan stopped. 'I didn't expect anything. Which is exactly what I got.'

'Look, Stefan,' Johnny said. 'This wasn't me. I didn't beat you up – it was Liam.'

From behind they heard someone shout, 'Blubber!'

Liam Clark had been joined by his mates. They were bouncing off each other like overheated molecules.

Stefan carried on walking without looking back.

'Earthquake warning!'

The group ran up and Liam booted Stefan's legs from behind. His knees buckled and he fell forward on to the pavement.

They ran off laughing.

'You OK?' Johnny bent over him.

'Get off me!' Stefan shouted. 'Just go away.' He got up, wiped his hands on his trousers and walked into school.

Phoebe came up behind Johnny.

'What was that about?'

Johnny hesitated. She was going out with Liam. Maybe she would side with him.

He shrugged. 'You know what Liam's like,' he said.

'Well, I thought I did. But obviously not.' She sighed. 'I'm new here too, you know. I joined the school at Easter. And no one thought to tell me that Liam's a psycho. I mean, what reason would he have for doing something like that?'

Johnny shrugged. 'I s'pose he enjoys it.'

Phoebe shook her head. 'How? Why? Arrrgghh! Boys – what is the matter with them?' she shouted as she ran off into school.

Johnny and Stefan had to sit together in Maths, but Stefan angled his chair so he was facing slightly away from him. In History they were supposed to work together on some questions, and Johnny tried, but when Stefan wouldn't answer him, he gave up and the pair worked separately.

At lunchtime Johnny sat alone, like he had done before, while Stefan was surrounded by people asking him about his black eye.

Then there was another rehearsal.

Johnny tried again in the changing room, making sure that his chest was out of sight as he got into his PE kit.

'I'm sorry about not being there to help you.'

'Yeah, bet you are,' Stefan said and walked off.

'Hey, you spoke!'

The door slammed shut in his face.

Johnny went to follow him, but then Stefan came back into the changing room.

'I don't really blame you, all right? No one wants to be beaten up. I get that. I just thought you were different, that's all.'

'I am,' said Johnny. He couldn't help his hand touching his chest. He had never felt so different.

Stefan shook his head. 'You're not, actually. You're just trying to fit in like everyone else.'

'Well, what if I am? What's wrong with that?'

Stefan raised his thick dark eyebrows. 'No one ever fits in, Johnny. Not really. Don't you know that? It's just that some people are better at pretending than others.'

Somehow Stefan had made him feel like an idiot, but Johnny wanted things to be right between them again, so he changed the subject. 'What did your dad say when he saw your eye?'

Stefan paused. 'He asked me what happened and I told him the truth. He tried to be nice about it, but I know he was disappointed in me.'

'But it wasn't your fault.'

'You know, it probably was,' said Stefan.

'How come?'

'For choosing friends who walk out on me the moment I need them.'

He turned and went into the gym.

That day Mrs Cray didn't put the music on straight away.

'Gather round,' she said. 'Before we begin, I have something for you to think about. Some of you have been studying *Animal Farm* in English, I believe?'

A few people nodded.

'OK. Well, I want you all to consider this: *Swan Lake* isn't really about swans any more than *Animal Farm* is about animals.'

153

Someone said, 'So what's it about then, ducks?'

Everyone laughed.

'No, it's not about ducks either.'

'Geese?' someone else suggested.

Mrs Cray rocked backwards and forwards on her huge strong feet. 'Does anyone else have any ideas?'

Phoebe looked quickly over to the back of the group, where Liam was standing.

'I think it's about belonging,' she said. 'You know, finding out who you are and which group you fit into.'

Mrs Cray beamed. 'That's right. The Prince wants to join in with the swans because they're offering him something that's lacking in his life: a place where he can feel himself. Now, I want you all to think about the swans as if they're people the next time you're dancing.'

'I've got an idea,' said Jonas. 'Why don't we save time and just say that? Why do we have to do all this prancing about?'

Mrs Cray fixed him with her sharp brown eyes. 'Because we all understand things better when we are shown them.'

She put the music on.

'So, scene three.' She turned to Johnny. 'My Prince, you've been rejected by your mother, and, following an embarrassing situation at a nightclub, you've gone to the park.' Her eyes sparkled, and she swept her arm towards the others. 'But this flock of majestic swans is so captivating that you forget your problems, and your only wish is to fly with them.'

Johnny looked over at the group. Flabby and greasy, in mismatched PE kits, they didn't look majestic or captivating to him.

154

'We're going to fly?' asked Lola.

Mrs Cray smiled. 'Yes!'

'But how? With ropes and harnesses and stuff?'

Mrs Cray shook her head. 'Feel your muscles, everyone.'

They all grabbed their puny biceps; a couple of the beefier students flexed their arms and made the muscles wriggle.

'Now imagine for a moment the arm strength needed to lift your body right up into the air.'

'Easy,' said a kid with freckles. 'I do pull-ups every day on a bar at home.'

'Good,' said Mrs Cray. 'But are you strong enough to fly? Go on, try.'

They all just stared at her, so she started running around the room, slowly moving her arms up and down like wings.

'Come on!' she called. 'Join in! It's wonderful!'

She looked mad, but one by one they followed her, jogging and flapping and squawking and messing around.

After a lap or two, the circle of flapping bodies gradually became more uniform; the up and down movement of their arms synchronised with the music that was now playing.

'Higher!' shouted Mrs Cray. 'Up! Up! Up! Come on!'

Johnny ran around with Phoebe and Stefan, and he could suddenly feel how strong his arms were – maybe not strong enough to get him off the ground, but strong enough for it to feel possible.

'Forget your hands. You don't have hands – they're wing tips,' Mrs Cray shouted.

Then, simultaneously, some of them began leaping as well as running, forming an outer ring, a fast lane.

'Shoulders down, and long necks like swans! Strength! I want to see the strength! Show me the power behind those wings.' Mrs Cray was yelling like a lunatic.

Power. Johnny was used to feeling weak.

But now he felt powerful.

'Conquer the air!'

Yes! The air was as thick as water, and Johnny was mastering it, using it to propel himself on and up.

And then he remembered something.

When he was little they had an old concrete coal bunker in the garden. When no one was looking, Johnny would scramble on top of it and jump off, flapping his arms like mad, convinced that it would work, that he would be able to fly.

He was disappointed every time that he fell to the ground, but he didn't give up. Not until the day his dad saw him doing it.

'You might as well stop that now, Johnny,' he'd said. 'I don't want you to break your neck. Boys can't fly.'

'Johnny, could you leave the circle, please.'

Johnny woke from the memory and Mrs Cray led him to the corner.

'Have you been practising your leap?'

Johnny nodded. 'A bit.'

'Good, because it's the closest any human being can come to flying without equipment. If you get it right, you'll soar right across the stage.'

Ignoring the others who were still flying around, they began to run and leap together. Mrs Cray was still better than Johnny. She was fluid and strong. It was like her leaps were just an extension of herself.

'Not bad, Johnny,' she said after the fifth jump. 'You're nearly there.'

'Nearly?' Johnny was leaning over, his hands on his knees, panting. 'I thought that was pretty good.'

'Yes, it was pretty good. But it wasn't perfect. Well, not in the sense I'm looking for. It's still missing something. Don't worry, it'll come – if you want it enough.'

He did. He wanted it enough. But wanting didn't seem to make it any easier.

She put her hand on his arm. 'We'll be doing the final scene tomorrow. That's when you'll need it, so keep practising. Leap as if your life depends on it.'

Liam was waiting when Phoebe came out of the girls' changing room.

He looked different, anxious maybe. But that wasn't her problem any more.

'Wanna meet up after school?' he asked her.

She nearly walked on past him. But instead she stopped, took a breath and asked, 'Did you beat up Stefan?'

The corners of Liam's mouth twitched as he scanned her face.

'Why d'you ask that?'

'Did you?'

Liam put his head to one side and widened his eyes, but even his 'cute face' didn't remind her why she had agreed to go out with him.

'Go on, Phoebe, let's meet up. I'll take you somewhere nice. Have a burger or pizza if you want. I've got money.'

Phoebe pulled herself up to her full height, which made her taller than Liam, and shook her head.

'Not if you were the last kid in school.'

As she walked off she heard him shouting, 'Why? What have I done?'

And the sound of him kicking a bin.

Phoebe walked on alone.

Mojo was first out of the door, holding a scarf, when Johnny collected him from school.

'It's my lead. I found it in Lost Property. Put it on please.'

Johnny tied the scarf around his tiny wrist, and Mojo started to pull Johnny down the road.

'Heel, Mojo!'

'But you said we could go to the park, and I want to hurry up so I can play with the pit balls,' he said.

'OK, but they're bulls, not balls. You even know what pit bulls are?' Johnny asked, laughing.

'Yes, they're little balls you jump into at a ball pit.'

'That wasn't quite what I meant. But you can build a sandcastle instead.'

There were two parks nearby. But the closer one had *KEEP OFF* tape over most of the play equipment, which made it look like a crime scene. So they walked on further, to the playground at Primrose Hill, where most of the children were looked after by nannies, ate dried seaweed instead of crisps and had names that Johnny didn't know could be names.

But first they stopped at the top of the hill to watch the kite flyers and look out over the city.

Mojo pointed to the London Zoo aviary, visible in the distance.

'Can we go there?'

'Not today,' Johnny said. 'It's too expensive, but I'll ask Mum to start saving the tokens on the cereal packets so we can get in for free.'

Mojo spoke to a pigeon pecking the ground near his

feet. 'Don't go down there, little bird! You don't want to get caught and put in that net!'

Johnny laughed. 'I don't think they're interested in pigeons at the zoo.'

Mojo stood up. 'I'll race you to the play park!'

Johnny let him win. At the bottom, Mojo slipped his lead and went to make sandcastles with lolly-stick flag-poles and old seaweed packets to line the moat.

Johnny sat on a nearby bench and shut his eyes for a moment. The sun was warm on his face and he was just drifting off when he heard a terrible yell.

He snapped his eyes open.

Mojo was sitting on top of a little girl. He was growling and his eyes were angry and terrified at the same time. The girl was yelling and struggling, but Mojo didn't seem able to move.

Johnny ran over and picked him up.

Mojo didn't react for a moment. A woman had scooped up the girl and was hugging and shushing her.

'Sorry, I didn't see what happened. He's not usually like that,' Johnny lied. There was no 'usually' for Mojo any more.

The woman turned to him. 'Don't worry, love, it was probably six of one and half a dozen of the other . . .' She looked puzzled. 'Johnny, isn't it?'

He recognised her then. She was one of the police officers who had come to their house after his dad died.

She was trying to smile at him, but he could see her memory of that day through her blue eyes.

The body lying just outside on Timbuktu Street.

The visit to break the news to his family.

The way his mum screamed and then shouted.

How he and Mojo were silent.

Johnny saw the pity on her face, and he felt embarrassed and then furious. Why was she there, reminding him of that day? What right did she have to barge into his life and make him feel awful again?

'How are things? Mojo's really grown. And so have you! And how's your mum?' She had hardly taken a breath.

'I'm sorry,' he said, grabbing Mojo, 'you've got the wrong person. C'mon, M—' He made up a different name. 'C'mon, Milo, we're late.'

That night Johnny dreamt that he was in his old bedroom. But it was cold, and the wallpaper was peeling off the walls and the carpets had been ripped out.

He heard a hard knock at the door, and he looked through the window.

It was the police.

Johnny ran downstairs.

His mum was by the door, just about to open it.

He tried to tell her not to, because if she didn't then maybe his dad wouldn't be dead, but the only sound he could make was a quiet hiss, and his mum thought he was messing around.

He screamed as she turned the door handle . . .

Johnny opened his eyes.

A soft light was coming in from the kitchen. He thought his mum must be awake, but when he went to see, it wasn't her.

Mojo was at the table with a pen in his hand, staring at it.

'Mojo,' Johnny tried to whisper, but nothing at all came out.

'Mo-jo.' This time he shouted, and, though it was as loud as he could manage, his voice was husky and still barely audible.

Mojo looked up, frowning.

'You don't sound like you any more,' he said.

'Well, I am me.'

'Why is your voice so funny then?'

'It's not,' Johnny said.

But he knew that it was. It was raspy, and quiet. Like the call of a mute swan.

Oh great, he thought.

Mojo smiled. 'If you're losing your voice you won't be able to tell Mum that I was up in the middle of the night drawing, will you?'

'I can still talk,' Johnny rasped.

'You won't tell her, will you? Not 'til it's finished?'

As Johnny shook his head, Mojo stretched out his little finger.

Johnny curled his own smallest finger around it. Mojo's dark eyes were deep and urgent.

'Pinkie promise?' Mojo said. 'You really won't tell her? No matter what? Not 'til I say you can?'

'Course I won't,' whispered Johnny.

'Then say it.'

He sighed. 'OK. I, Johnny Emin, pinkie promise not to tell Mum about the table until you say so.'

They squeezed their fingers together.

'Is that all right now?' Johnny said.

Mojo nodded. 'Yes. I trust you. Don't let me down.'

Johnny laughed. 'Good. Now come on, let's go to bed.'

Mojo fell asleep in seconds.

But Johnny was wide awake, afraid to sleep in case he had another nightmare.

When he finally slept, he dreamt that he was dancing down the street with Mrs Cray. They were doing really

complicated steps that he had never seen before but somehow he knew them.

Then she said, 'Are you ready?'

He nodded, and they leapt up and into the sky, and he
could fly.

He could really fly!

But just when Johnny got so high that he could feel the
damp clouds on his face, his mum called his name and he
plummeted back towards earth.

Chapter Twelve

Tuesday

Johnny woke just before he hit the ground.

His heart was banging in his chest, and he knew that he would never get back to sleep.

So, although it was only six o'clock, he went into the bathroom, and, as he had done every day since the feathers first grew, he took off his T-shirt and looked in the mirror.

There they were: a thin covering as white and beautiful as ever.

Johnny stroked the down on his chest, like he might have stroked a cat.

A cat that he was about to put down.

His mum's pink razor was still there. He had to do it. He'd been lucky so far, but someone was bound to notice soon. And then ... well, he couldn't even consider that.

Johnny picked up the razor and started scraping it over his chest, beginning at the bottom, a few centimetres from his belly button, and working his way up. But the feathers were tougher than they looked and dragged painfully against the blade, making his chest bleed.

Johnny gave up, threw the razor back in the sink and stared at himself in the mirror.

His face had changed so much recently that he hardly recognised himself, and he wasn't sure how he felt about it.

His jaw was stronger and his face had lost the roundness of a child's. His nose had grown too, and if he put his hand to his neck he could feel his Adam's apple.

Other than the feathers, the biggest change was the hair. And it was the only one he could do anything about.

He went to look for Mojo's stash of pens. They were still on the table from the night before.

Curious about what he had been drawing, Johnny peeled back the tablecloth.

Mojo's illustrations were now covering more than half the table. There were scenes and people, like a comic strip but with only a few words.

He covered it over again, then took a black felt-tip pen away with him into the bathroom. The white streak shone out like the swans' feathers had done across the lake. He pushed the thought from his mind and started colouring in.

At first he got more on his fingers than on the hair, but in the end all the white was covered. His hair was back to normal.

Black.

Then he settled down on the sofa to watch morning TV.

His mum came in, yawning. 'Johnny, what are you doing up so early?'

'Nothing.' He sat up, yawned too.

She frowned, then walked right over to him.

'Look at this black stuff! What exactly have you been doing to your hair? Is that pen?'

There was a dark smudge on the fabric of the sofa.

'And how am I supposed to get that out?' She sighed. 'Oh, I see. So this is what it's all about then.' She looked away from him as if she were addressing an audience. 'I do know what's going on, Johnny. I suppose it's inevitable.'

Inevitable?

What did she mean?

Was she saying the thing that Johnny had hardly dared to think since the feathers first appeared?

That he might be turning into a swan?

'But you don't have to put up with it,' Mum continued.

He didn't?

'It's obvious you're being bullied, Johnny. Is it because of the hair? Or is it the dance show? Because you know that they're just jealous about you having the lead part, don't you?'

Oh. So it wasn't about turning into a swan.

Johnny let out a deep breath. 'It's nothing to do with school, Mum.' His voice was quiet and husky. 'Nobody did anything to me.'

'Eh?' she said. 'I can hardly hear you.'

'Nobody did anything to me,' he repeated. His voice was still rasping.

'Johnny, the clothes you were wearing to school on Wednesday – they were wet through, and they smelled of stagnant water.'

Johnny had meant to rinse them out.

'Did someone push you in a pond or something?'

'No, Mum.'

'Well, how did they get wet then?'

He shrugged, then winced. 'I went swimming.'

'What? In a pond?' His mum sighed again. 'Look, Johnny, I understand that you don't want to tell tales on anyone, but pushing someone in a pond is dangerous.'

'In a lake, Mum,' he said. 'It was a lake, not a pond. And no one pushed me. But don't worry, I get it. No more lakes.'

'But why would you anyway? It doesn't make any sense. If you want to go swimming there's a leisure centre down the road.'

'I know. Look, I'm sorry, it was a spur-of-the-moment thing. It was stupid, and I won't do it again.'

She pursed her lips, then said, 'Promise?'

'Yes, I just said, didn't I?'

Johnny went into the bathroom and looked at his hair in the mirror. Some of the pen had rubbed off and it had gone a light grey colour. It looked like he was ready to go trick-or-treating.

He rubbed shampoo into his fringe and rinsed it, leaning over the bath. The ink washed out, leaving his streak not quite white.

He felt sorry that he had ruined it.

Mojo was sitting in the kitchen eating his breakfast.

'I had a look at the table just now,' Johnny whispered to him. 'It's getting pretty full.'

Mojo stopped eating. 'I'm stuck. I don't know how to do the middle.' He stared at the tablecloth as if he could see through it.

'I know what I said last night,' said Johnny. 'But this cloth's getting dirty, and Mum will take it off to wash it soon. Why don't we get rid of the drawings before she gets a chance to see? I'm sure they'll come off with bleach.'

'No. Not 'til I've finished.'

Johnny poured himself some cereal, added milk and took a big spoonful.

'How about I promise to bring you back a really big piece of paper tonight? And you can copy it all on to there? I'll even help you. Then we'll scrub it off the table before Mum gets back.'

Mojo turned on him, baring his tiny teeth.

'Not. Til. I've. Finished!' he shouted and deliberately knocked his bowl off the table.

'What did you do that for?' Johnny said. 'You're a nutter, you know that?' He got a cloth from the sink and threw it at Mojo. 'Here, you can clean that up yourself. I was only trying to help.'

He heard a sniffing sound. Tears were pouring down Mojo's cheeks. 'Will you, Johnny? Will you help me?'

'Yeah, I've already said I would. We can start copying it tonight.'

'No. Not about the table. I want you to help me find Dad.'

Johnny's body stiffened. 'You can't,' he said. 'He's gone, Mojo. We can't see him.'

'Has our house gone too?'

'No. Well, I don't think so. I expect it's still there. But he's not in it.'

'Well, if he's not there, where is he?'

'He's, erm . . .'

Mojo hadn't gone to the funeral. Mum said he was too young.

Johnny hadn't had any choice though.

On the day his dad was buried he had tried to stay in bed. He told everyone he was sick. But one of his mum's sisters, down from Scotland, had come into the room, shut the door behind her and perched on the end of his bed.

'It's hard and it's not fair,' she had told him. 'But,

Johnny, your dad's gone, so you're the man of the house. That's just the way it is.'

Johnny had kept his head under the covers to muffle the sound of his crying.

'Your mum and Mojo are going to need your support. That's your job now. And, well, today's the day that job starts.' His aunt gently put her hand on his leg. 'You can do it, Johnny. I know you can. Now climb into your suit and get yourself downstairs.'

So he'd put on the stiff new clothes and pretended he was OK.

And when he heard the big black car of death coming down the road, instead of running away, he had taken his mum's arm and got into the hearse to travel his dad's last half a mile with him.

He had kept hold of her arm while they sat on the cold chapel bench and watched his dad disappear.

'He's near the house,' Johnny told Mojo now.

'Take me to see him.' Mojo grabbed his hand. 'Please take me to see him.'

The receptionist at Mojo's school didn't like Johnny much, and she was even less pleased to see him than usual.

'Shouldn't you be in school?' she hissed through the glass, glancing at the inspectors who were taking notes.

'Mum has sent me to pick up Mojo for the dentist,' he told her, his voice still croaky. 'She couldn't park, so I'm here to get him.'

The receptionist frowned and checked a large black book.

'No, I haven't got it written down. You'll have to get your mum to come and authorise it.'

'She can't. She's on double yellow lines and she says we can't afford to pay another parking ticket.'

'Can't she phone?'

'No. She's got no credit. That's why she sent me in.'

The receptionist glared at him, jaw clenched, eyes sliding over towards the suited men.

'We do ask that dental appointments are made for after-school hours, you know,' she said unnaturally loudly.

'Yes, but it's an emergency. Mojo's got really bad toothache, and it's been stopping him sleeping. He's in awful pain. And it's really affecting his behaviour.' Johnny impressed himself with how good he was at lying. 'At school,' he added.

The receptionist looked over towards the men in suits, then made a call, whispering into the mouthpiece.

'I've asked someone to send him straight up,' she said, putting the phone down.

A moment later, Mojo appeared, grinning widely.

'Hold your cheek,' Johnny whispered.

Mojo clamped his hand to his face.

The receptionist gave him a fake sympathetic smile and a thumbs up as she buzzed the door open.

Taking Mojo by the hand, Johnny led him out of the school and down the road to Swiss Cottage Tube station. But Mojo baulked at the steps that descended into the ticket hall.

'I don't want to go down under the ground.'

'It's just the Tube, Mojo. You used to go on the Tube all the time. Don't you remember?'

Mojo shook his head and repeated, 'I don't want to go under the ground.'

Johnny sighed. 'It's perfectly safe.'

'No,' said Mojo, and he sat down on the top step.

'Are you seriously going to do this?' Johnny asked.

'I'm not going down there.'

Johnny checked his watch and his pockets. They didn't have enough time to take the bus, or enough money for a taxi.

'Sorry, we have no choice,' he said. 'The only way to get there is by . . .' He had an idea. 'By dragon.'

'Dragon? But you said Tube.'

'No, I didn't. I said dragon. You just weren't listening properly. Dragon is the only way to travel back in time.'

'Back in time?'

'Yes. That's what we're doing today.'

'Really?'

'Of course.'

'And the dragon lives in there?'

'Yes. Down those steps.'

'Will it eat us?' Mojo's eyes were wide, but he was smiling.

'Nah. That's just what happens in books. Dragons are pretty tame nowadays. Vegetarians, mostly.'

Mojo smiled. 'OK.'

'OK?'

'Yes, OK. Let's go, Johnny!'

Mojo pulled Johnny down into the station, where they bought tickets from the machine and waited on the platform. He gripped Johnny's hand tightly as it became more and more crowded, and the electronic board counted down the minutes until the train was due.

'What does it say?' Mojo asked. 'What are those numbers?'

'It's how many dragons are around,' Johnny told him.

'Wow! Six!' Mojo frowned. 'Oh, no, only five dragons now.'

'That's OK. When there's only one dragon left it means that it's ours and it's coming to get us.'

After that, Mojo watched the board, ignoring the crowds around him, until finally there was a rumble in the distance.

'It's nearly here,' Johnny said. 'And it's a bit scary, so close your eyes and I'll lead you deep into its belly.'

Mojo squeezed his eyes shut and clenched his jaw.

There was a rumbling roar and he gripped Johnny's hand tighter. Then a whoosh of dusty air, scented with electricity, blew their hair back as the Tube train arrived.

'Ready?'

Mojo nodded.

'Then let's enter the belly of the beast,' said Johnny, and they were sucked aboard with the crowds.

There were no seats. But Johnny realised with surprise that he was now tall enough to reach the yellow hand-rail above his head. The one that his dad used to hang on to with one arm, while holding him tight with the other.

'OK, you can open your eyes.'

Mojo scanned the carriage and smiled. 'Hey, dragon guts look exactly like the inside of a train!'

'*Oh, Danny Boy, the pipes, the pipes are calling!*' A home-less man was coming down the carriage, singing a drunken song.

'Please?' Mojo asked.

'OK.' Johnny found 50p in his pocket, and he let Mojo put it in the man's outstretched hat.

It was what his dad would have done.

'It's great inside the dragon,' Mojo shouted over the whine and clatter.

The man heard him and switched to singing 'Puff the Magic Dragon'.

But Johnny wasn't listening.

A group had come into the carriage. The girls had their hair in buns, and they carried tote bags with a ballet shoe logo.

The boys, only a few years older than Johnny, stood just in front of him, and he couldn't help staring at the way they stood and watching the muscles in their arms as they held on to the rails while the train jolted.

He imagined them dancing *Swan Lake*, with their strong, upright bodies. He thought about himself – his own body, so weak in comparison – and he felt ashamed even to be trying.

'Why are you staring at them, Johnny?' Mojo asked.

The man had stopped singing and moved on.

Johnny flushed. 'Shut up. I'm not staring.'

'You were,' said Mojo.

But then the students got off, laughing at some joke one of them had made, and Johnny was left looking at his own reflection in the darkened glass, his white streak shining and his worried eyes like coals.

At London Bridge Johnny led Mojo, his eyes closed, from one Tube line to the next. Then a few stops later, the two emerged into the daylight at Tooting station.

'You ready to go back in time, Mojo?'

'Yes,' said Mojo. 'To the Pyramids?'

'No, not ancient Egypt.'

'Where then?'

'We're visiting our past, Mojo. First stop, Timbuktu Road.'

'Our old house?' Mojo whispered.

Johnny nodded. 'Our old home. Come on.'

Mojo skipped as they went down the high street.

Not much had changed – it had only been a few months since they had left – but it all felt foreign to Johnny, like it didn't fit him any more.

When he saw the sign, they turned left on to their street. The terraces curved around, with houses on both sides a mix of red brick and painted render.

Here it felt like they had never gone away. The shapes, the colours, the smells – everything was as he remembered it.

The gutters were strewn with rubbish, grass poked up between the paving slabs, and the rusted old cars up on bricks were bumper to bumper with smarter, newer models.

Johnny thought it was beautiful.

'This way. Just up here. Number forty-eight. Right at the top, with the old lamp post outside.'

'Will another family be living there?' Mojo asked, just like Johnny had asked his mum.

'I don't know. Maybe. So we can't go in.'

'Rufus!'

Mojo pulled his hand away from Johnny's, and ran up to a white cat that was sitting on a wall cleaning itself.

'Can I stroke him?' he asked.

'No, he bites. Remember?'

But Mojo didn't answer, and suddenly Johnny couldn't talk either, because they had both spotted number forty-eight.

Mojo took a step backwards. 'That's not our house.'

'No!' breathed Johnny, checking the ones on either side to be sure.

He stepped closer, unable to take it all in.

The grass and flowers in the front garden had gone. In their place were dark purple slate chips and big terracotta plant pots with jungle ferns growing inside.

The white render, painted every year by his dad from a tall ladder, was now grey, a pale shade too close to white to be sure of itself.

Their front door had been replaced. The new one was made from strips of varnished wood, with a porthole window at the top and an oversized steel handle.

But the worst thing of all was the windows.

Their rattly wooden sashes with rippled Victorian glass were no more. In their place was metal-framed double glazing which bounced the light back flatly.

It was like the house had been blinded.

Johnny made a decision.

'No,' he said to Mojo, 'that's definitely not our house.'

Mojo looked relieved. 'So where's it gone then?'

Johnny didn't want him to have to face up to the truth: that someone had thought the house they loved wasn't good enough. So they had ripped the heart out of it.

He tutted and shook his head. 'We must've arrived just too late. I thought it was going tomorrow,' said Johnny.

'Going where?'

'Oh, our house has been transported by hot-air balloon to a really nice street, so it can have a much bigger garden.'

Mojo looked unsure.

'Big enough for a climbing frame with a slide,' Johnny added.

'Really?'

'Of course. And a swing.'

'Can we go and find it?'

'Yes. Soon. But not today, Mojo. We're in a hurry now. We're going . . .'

And maybe this was the point when Johnny should have taken Mojo back to the Tube and forgotten about the real reason for the trip. But he didn't.

He said, 'We're going to see Dad.'

★　　　★　　　★

Lambeth Cemetery was only a five-minute walk, but they were silent all the way.

Johnny knew that Mojo hadn't believed his story about the house being taken away any more than he had believed in the dragon, but he hoped it had made things easier, because the next bit was going to be even worse.

They walked through the stone archway and surveyed the lines and lines of graves, standing like forgotten teeth.

Mojo's mouth hung open.

'What is this place?'

'It's the cemetery. It's where people go when they die.'

Mojo shook his head. 'But there are so many! They can't all be dead.'

'This way, down here.'

Johnny led him to the family grave. The one he had visited when only his grandparents were buried there.

'We're here,' he said.

They had stopped at a white marble gravestone, with soft, greyish-green blooms of moss scattered over the lettering.

His grandparents' names and dates were at the top, and his dad's were carved in smaller letters at the bottom.

Like a PS.

JEM EMIN
Beloved son and father
1976–2015

Mojo stared at it for a second, then looked away, tilting his face to the sky.

A single large white bird flew above them and they watched until it was out of sight.

Johnny hoped that the Buddhists were right, and that his dad was now a skylark or a dolphin, or even a rat or an earwig.

Anything would be better than being dead and buried.

Johnny put his arms round Mojo and felt his warmth.

'Is he really in there?' Mojo asked, still looking up at the clouds.

'Yes, he's under the ground, with his own dad.'

'Because he's dead? Because his heart was broken?'

Johnny sighed. 'Yes.'

Mojo slowly lowered his gaze and looked at Johnny. His eyes seemed too big for his pale face. He looked terrified.

What had Johnny done?

The whole thing was a mistake.

First the house, then this.

He had thought Mojo needed to see it. To understand. If he didn't see for himself he would never believe it, never move on from Stage One, denial; never get back to how he used to be. Mrs Cray had said that people understand better if you show them.

But all that Johnny had done was ruin their memories for ever.

Mojo's eyes moved to the grave. 'Right under the ground? Are you sure? With all the dirt and the worms?'

'Yes.'

It was too late to change it now. He would have to try and make it better.

Johnny knelt down beside him and held his hand. The way that his dad had held his hand at the Eiffel Tower.

'But he's in a box, Mojo,' he said. 'A really nice box. Mum chose it specially. It has a soft lining and shiny handles. He's . . .'

But then from nowhere Johnny started to cry, and it swallowed up his hoarse voice and left him with nothing but sobs.

Mojo patted his back. 'It's OK, Johnny. Just wait here.' And he stepped right up to the gravestone.

'Daddy,' Johnny heard him whisper. Then Mojo put his arms around the cold, hard gravestone and hugged it. 'I do love you. I'm sorry. I'm really, really sorry, Daddy.'

In the Tube on the way back, Mojo put his head on Johnny's shoulder. 'He's never coming back, is he?'

Johnny pulled him close. 'No, he's never coming back.'

They were silent for a moment.

Then Mojo said, 'So how will we find our house?'

He had believed the story, and Johnny was glad.

'Well, we'll recognise it when we see it, I s'pose. It'll feel right. Like home.'

Mojo thought for a minute. 'But I can't really remember what it used to look like. Can you tell me?'

Johnny shut his eyes, like he had done that day in the dance lesson, and he pictured it.

The squeaky gate with the silver latch.

The concrete path springing with hairy moss.

The neatly cut privet hedge running alongside.

And the white-painted pebble-dash that grazed your skin if you brushed against it.

'You can start with the front door,' said Mojo. 'What colour was it?'

'Red,' Johnny said. 'The front door was red.'

'Oh, yes. I remember now.'

'And we had a gold lion-head knocker.'

'And the birdbath that no birds went in,' Mojo said. 'Why didn't they go in it?'

177

'Too many cats. Especially Rufus – he's a killer.'

'And d'you remember the sound of the doorbell?' Mojo asked.

'*Bing-bing-bing-bong!*' They made the noise together, and then laughed.

They fell silent for a moment, then Mojo asked, 'Will we ever go home?'

'We're going home now,' Johnny said.

'Yes, but I mean back to our old life.'

Johnny thought about it.

'No,' he said. 'I'm sorry. Our old life is finished.'

Chapter Thirteen

It was three thirty by the time they stepped out of the Tube and into the early summer sunshine.

'Do we have to go back to school now?' Mojo asked.

'No. We can go home. But you mustn't tell Mum where we went. OK?'

'OK. Can we run back? I want to do my drawing.'

'You want to run, really?' Johnny was amazed at how quickly Mojo's mood had improved.

He smiled. 'Yeah.'

'Do you want me to teach you a special run?'

'OK.'

'Copy what I do.'

Still holding hands, Johnny showed Mojo some steps from *Swan Lake*.

'Think you can do that?'

'Course. Easy.'

They danced along, Mojo grinning and laughing. It was the happiest Johnny had seen him for ages.

'Perfect. Now let's add this.' He put a small leap into the routine, and they carried on down the road.

As they rounded a corner they stopped.

In front of them two groups of boys were facing each other.

In one group were Liam Clark and the Populars.

And, opposite them, were Stefan and the Leftovers.

'Swan Boy!' shouted Liam. 'How sweet – skipping down the road with little Cygnet Boy!'

'What's going on?' Johnny asked Stefan.

'Nothing,' he said. 'Go home.'

Johnny held Mojo's hand tighter.

'Tell me.'

'Nothing, I said. Just take your brother home.'

Johnny looked down at Mojo. He'd seen too much that day already.

But he couldn't leave Stefan.

Not twice.

'Go, Swan Boy!' Liam said again. 'It's not your fight. Me and Stefan just need to have a chat about our business arrangement.'

'Ah, get lost, Clark. I owe you nothing,' said Stefan, stepping forward.

'Not according to my accounts,' said Liam.

The rest of the Leftovers stayed where they were. They may have even stepped backwards.

'Well, this is escalating quickly.' Liam laughed, as Jonas grabbed Stefan round the neck.

They were about the same height, but where Stefan was bulk, Jonas was pure muscle.

'Who d'you think you're telling to get lost?' Liam shouted in Stefan's face.

'You!' croaked Stefan, his complexion turning the same burgundy colour as his school jumper.

In response Jonas squeezed him even tighter.

'Who?' Liam repeated. 'I didn't quite hear that.'

'You!' Stefan managed to croak again.

'Who? Me? Are you sure?'

Johnny had seen enough.

'It was you, Liam, you!' Johnny's voice echoed off the building. 'Wait back there,' he said, pushing Mojo towards the Leftovers.

Then he launched himself at Jonas.

'Let go of him!' Johnny was pulling at his massive arms. 'He can't breathe, you idiot.'

But Jonas just grinned. He was enjoying himself.

'Tell him to stop, Liam!' Johnny shouted. 'He's going to kill Stefan.'

Liam laughed. 'What's wrong? You don't want your little girlfriend to die?'

'Seriously, Liam,' said one of his friends. 'He's gone a funny colour.'

Liam nodded at Jonas. 'Let him go. He's learnt his lesson.' Then he turned towards Johnny. 'I don't think you have though. You still think you're something special. And you're not. So let's sort this out. You and me, one-to-one.'

Johnny looked Liam in the eye. He hadn't forgotten any of the times that Liam had hurt or humiliated him. But he wasn't scared any more.

He touched his chest where Liam had planted his boot. The feathers had covered the bruises, and his body had healed them.

Johnny had changed.

'Or are you chicken, Swan Boy?' Liam turned to his friends and grinned. 'Hey, that's a joke. Chicken, swan, geddit?'

Johnny seized his chance and lunged at Liam, acting on instinct – and it didn't feel like a human instinct that he could control.

181

Arm to arm.

Skin to skin.

Bones crashing against bones.

Pulling and punching.

No pain, no fear, just anger.

Boiling, burning rage.

'Go, Johnny!' He could hear the Leftovers yelling support. 'Kill him, Johnny!'

Liam was good at fighting, but Johnny could feel just how small he really was underneath his blows.

Johnny hit him three or four times, not letting him hit back, but, though Stefan and the others were cheering him on, the more he hit the less he wanted to.

'Johnny!' He could hear Mojo's high voice. 'Stop!'

He took one more shot, and then he let his arm fall.

'What a wimp!' jeered one of Liam's gang, half-heartedly.

'Go on!' yelled one of the Leftovers. 'You were beating him!'

But Johnny didn't care about beating the bullies any more.

He wasn't a wimp. Liam knew it now, but so did he. And that was what mattered.

'Let's go home,' said Mojo.

'Next time,' said Jonas.

'Shut up, Jonas,' said Liam. 'It's over. Just leave it.'

'What?'

'You heard me.'

Jonas looked like he was going to punch Liam. But instead he walked away.

Liam glared at Johnny, then hobbled off in the other direction.

'Where did that come from?' Stefan asked, his voice husky from the attack.

'Dunno.'

'Well, thanks for saving me and everything,' Stefan said, 'but d'you know you fight like my sister?'

'Worked though, didn't it?' Johnny said, starting to laugh. But then he stopped because out of the corner of his eye Johnny had seen something much more terrifying than Liam's gang.

His mum.

'I've gotta go,' he said. And he grabbed Mojo and walked up to her as normally as he could.

Johnny's mum's face was like a volcano about to explode. Lava was practically dripping from her lips.

'Home,' she said, and they walked along behind her.

Back at the flat, Johnny's mum finally erupted.

'Truanting! And then fighting – in the street! With your little brother watching!'

'I know! I know, I'm sorry. But if you listen, I can explain.'

'So, are these your new friends? The ones who encouraged you to jump in a pond?'

'It was a lake.'

Her eyes flared, sparks shooting from them. 'It's the same difference! So, what's the excuse? What possible reason did you have for taking Mojo out of school and having a street fight?'

'I did it for him!'

'For him?' His mum fake-laughed.

'Well, the first bit was for him; the next bit was for Stefan.'

She looked at him and shook her head.

'I don't even know who this Stefan is, but you should be ashamed of yourself, Johnny. You really should.'

183

'Maybe I should, but you know what? I'm not!' He stomped to the door and slammed it shut behind him.

Johnny sat at the bottom of the stairs and didn't know what to do. He put his hand in his pocket. He had no money, just his Tube ticket from earlier.

He set off in the direction of the station.

He would go and visit one of his old friends from Tooting.

Ronnie or Tagor or Yusuf or Will.

But he thought about it as he walked and his anger faded.

It was nearly five o'clock on a school day. He hadn't heard from them at all since he left, and he didn't know where they hung out nowadays. They could be anywhere and he didn't have a phone to call them and check. Anyway, what would he say to them? So much had happened that he wouldn't know where to begin.

He stopped walking and changed direction.

Johnny found Pete's Pizzas easily. It was a few shops down from the Best Kebab House. A bald man leant against the counter, picking his teeth with a cocktail stick. He was a bigger, smooth-headed version of Stefan.

As Johnny walked in, he smiled.

'Yes, young man?'

'Is Stefan here?'

'You a friend of his?'

'Yes.'

'Were you in that fight today?'

Johnny hung his head. 'Yeah,' he muttered.

'And did my boy fight bravely?'

Johnny thought of Stefan, his face puce as he struggled to breathe.

'Oh, yes,' he replied. 'You should see the other guy – he was a mess!'

Stefan's dad beamed.

'Then free garlic bread! On the house! Ste-fano!' he yelled.

Stefan came through the fly-strip curtain.

'All right, Johnny?'

'Yeah.'

'Here, take this.' Stefan's dad handed Johnny a warm paper bag. 'Enough for both of you. We're quiet at the moment, so you can go with your friend, Stefano. Be back before dark.'

Johnny held the bag tight as they walked out on to the street. 'So, where shall we go?'

'Somewhere with good views that will do justice to the experience that is my dad's garlic bread.'

'Follow me,' said Johnny. 'I know just the place.'

The lift in Burnham Tower was working again, and as they travelled up, Stefan said, 'So why won't you tell me where we're going? What's so special up here?'

The lift stopped.

'London,' said Johnny as the doors swept open. 'Welcome to your city.'

It was windy, and as they stepped out on to the roof Stefan gasped.

'This is amazing!' He started running around the roof-top, flapping his arms. 'Look at me, Mrs Cray, I'm flying!'

'Just keep away from the edge,' Johnny said.

'What? No, the edge is the best bit. Come up here with me.'

Stefan climbed on to the ledge and stood with his arms outstretched.

'I'm the King of London!' he shouted into the wind.

'Get down!'

'Nah. I used to do tightrope-walking. I love it up here.'

Stefan's phone played the first few notes from Beethoven's Fifth. '*Duh-duh-duh duuuhhhh.*'

He jumped down and answered the call.

'What's up, Phoebe?' He put his hand over the phone and looked at Johnny. 'Shall I invite her over?'

Johnny shrugged. 'Yeah, OK.'

'I'm not sharing the garlic bread though. I'm a growing boy.'

He gave Phoebe the address, then they sat down together with their backs against the barrier.

'Here.' Stefan passed him a piece of garlic bread and watched Johnny's face as he bit into it. 'The best, isn't it?'

'Yeah. Pretty good.' Johnny caught a trickle of green-speckled butter that was running down his chin. 'So, sounds like you told your dad about the fight.'

'Yeah. He was made up.'

Johnny laughed. 'My mum went mad.'

Stefan shrugged. 'Parents, eh? There's no point even trying to understand them.'

'D'you think it's over?' Johnny said. 'D'you think they'll leave us alone now?'

Stefan took another bite of garlic bread. 'Yeah, I think so. You won.'

'D'you reckon?'

Stefan laughed. 'Yeah. It'll be all over school already that you beat up Liam. No one's going to pick on you any more. In fact –' he took another bite of garlic bread – 'I'd say you're one of them now.'

Johnny shivered and wished he'd brought a jacket.

By the time Phoebe came up on to the roof, they had eaten all the garlic bread.

'You two stink,' she said, settling down next to them. 'So, what was this all about?'

She held out her phone and they watched the footage of the fight between Johnny and Liam.

'Who put it up?' asked Stefan.

'That's the strange thing,' said Phoebe. 'It was Jonas.'

'Jonas?' Johnny and Stefan said at the same time.

'Has the world gone mad?' asked Stefan.

Phoebe shook her head. 'Maybe it's always been mad,' she said. 'But we've only just noticed.'

It was nearly dark by the time Johnny went back downstairs. Mojo was in bed but his mum was sitting at the table next to a half-empty bottle of wine.

'I was worried.' She said it like an explanation, not an accusation.

'I'm sorry.'

'I'm sorry too,' she said. 'I didn't give you a chance to talk earlier.'

'No, you didn't.'

'So, are you going to tell me what happened?'

Johnny shrugged. 'I didn't mean to get into a fight. I just did what I thought was right. But it wasn't right. In fact, it was horrible. So I won't be doing it again.'

His mum put her arm around him.

'Good. It didn't seem like you. Maybe it's the other boys? That huge kid – he looked like a right one.'

Johnny shook his head. 'No, Stefan's not like that either.' He smiled. 'But don't tell his dad.'

'Well, as long as you've learnt a lesson, let's just forget it. But you do need to tell me why you took Mojo out of school.'

Johnny yawned. 'I will. Tomorrow.'

She put her head on one side, then said, 'All right then, I suppose it can wait.'

She gave him a hug.

'Ooh, you stink of garlic,' she said.

'And you stink of booze,' he replied.

She looked at the wine bottle and laughed. 'I expect I do. I'm going to pay for that tomorrow.'

'Yeah, you're not exactly setting me a good example, are you?'

She smiled. 'Not exactly.'

There was silence for a moment, then Johnny said, 'Has the world always been mad? Y'know, before Dad died it seemed so normal.'

'Yes, Johnny,' she said. 'Mad, wonderful, tragic, painful, joyful. It's all of those things. Always has been, always will be.'

Johnny thought about the feathers, and the fight, and Mojo and his dad.

'I would quite like it to be normal for a while,' he said.

'I'll put in a request,' she replied, and, rising a little unsteadily, she kissed the top of his head.

Johnny fell asleep quickly.

But Mojo waited until he heard his mum go to bed and start snoring gently, then he took the pens from under his pillow and went into the kitchen.

He pulled off the tablecloth and looked at what he had done.

There was a circle of white left in the centre of the table, the size of a football. *It should be enough space*, he thought.

It had to be enough.

He climbed up on to the table and took a pen top off with his teeth, then sat with his legs crossed, hunched over, drawing fast, not bothering to colour in or do joined-up writing.

He just had to get it out. Once it was out, his tummy would stop bubbling and he wouldn't want to scream and kick and escape. Maybe his teacher would stop telling him off and the other children would want to play with him.

But what about his mum and Johnny?

When they saw the table, would they hate him?

He had to risk it.

He had to give the table all his sadness.

He couldn't keep it inside any more. It was just too big.

Chapter Fourteen

Wednesday

'Aaaghh . . .' Johnny could hardly move his head the next morning.

The knuckles on his right hand were red and swollen, and he had a faint ring of grey around his eye, like he had looked through the end of a grimy telescope. He had seen a few things the day before, but none of them was celestial.

His mum was wearing jeans and a T-shirt.

'D'you want a lift to school today?' she asked him.

'Why? You not going to work?'

'No, day off. I've invited a couple of friends over for dinner on Friday night, so I thought I'd go and get some shopping, clean the flat a bit.'

'Friends? The ones from work you went out with?'

'Yes. The very same. Why, is that a problem?'

Johnny shrugged. 'I dunno, it's just that you never used to invite people over.'

'I did. Well, maybe not so much recently. Anyway, I thought I'd do something special for dinner.'

'What are they like, your friends?'

'They're . . .' She smiled. A real smile. 'They're fun. You'll like them.'

Mojo came to the door. He had black pen all over his hands.

His mum frowned. 'Mojo, how did you get your hands dirty while you slept?' She ruffled his hair. 'I don't know. You're one for St Jude, you are.'

'Hopeless cases?' Johnny asked.

'You got it in one.'

Mojo yawned wide. 'Where's my breakfast? I'm starving!'

'Gotta go.' Johnny kissed his mum on the cheek.

He ran to school.

Stefan and the Leftovers were waiting for him in the place usually occupied by Liam's gang. Phoebe was with them too.

'Swan Boy!' they yelled, and it wasn't an insult.

Johnny grinned.

'Hey,' said Stefan. Johnny could see red marks on his neck. 'How's the hero today?'

Johnny didn't answer because he saw Liam walking towards them, head down.

Liam shot a look at Phoebe, then walked straight past without a word.

Stefan whistled.

'I wouldn't get used to Liam leaving us alone,' said Johnny. 'It's only because he's by himself. He's always braver when he's got backup.'

'Maybe, but look – there's Jonas now. What's he doing walking in with that lot?'

Coming along the road was a group of kids that Johnny thought of as the Wannabe Populars. Jonas was in the middle of them, and he looked happy.

'Weird!' said Stefan.

Just as Liam had done, Jonas looked away as he came closer.

'You know what,' said Stefan. 'I definitely think we've won.'

'Won?' Johnny shook his head. 'Won what? The right not to be beaten up?'

Stefan shrugged. 'Yeah. And I can keep my money too. It's all I've ever wanted.'

'Yeah, it's good,' said Johnny. 'I s'pose.'

But it didn't feel particularly good.

As they headed into school a Year Nine barged into him with his rucksack. He turned and looked at Johnny.

'Really sorry, mate,' he said. The boy spoke to his friends, then they all turned and stared at Johnny.

'See that!' said Stefan. 'Word has got around quickly. I s'pose the video helped. I'm glad there's no footage of me and Jonas though. That would've been embarrassing.'

Johnny shook his head. 'It's all embarrassing, Stefan.'

'No, it's not. Not for you. You're not just Swan Boy any more. You're a hero now. It's like in *Swan Lake*: you're royalty!'

Stefan called out to a group of Year Eights. 'Hey, you lot. D'you know who this kid is?'

They all nodded. 'Johnny Emin,' they said.

'See?' Stefan said. 'From now on, it's easy street for you, your majesty. And, as your trusted companion, for me too.'

The boys carried on looking at Johnny.

His new persona was reflected in their faces.

And Johnny realised something.

They looked at him the same way everyone used to look at Liam.

*　　*　　*

When Johnny walked into the gym for the rehearsal, there was a large table in the middle of the room.

'Ah, Johnny, I'm glad you've joined us today,' said Mrs Cray. 'You're just in time to die,' she added, in a loud, theatrical voice. 'And this is your deathbed.'

'Great,' said Johnny. 'Today's just getting better and better.'

'Hop up, and while I teach the swans their dance, I'd like you to think about how you want to do this.'

Johnny thought that right now he'd very much like to shut his eyes and forget the show and school and everything else. His body ached from the fight and he felt wrong inside.

He didn't feel like himself any more.

Not that the bullied Swan Boy was himself, but nor was someone that beat other people up in the street.

He lay on the hard table, and, half-listening to Mrs Cray ('Straight backs, and left-and-right-and-left-and-right, long necks!'), he wondered what it was like to die.

His dad hadn't known it was coming. One moment he was at home giving Mojo his dinner, and the next he was on his way to the corner shop when he collapsed in the street. No illness, no oncoming car, no looking down the barrel of a gun.

Just normal life and then
    nothing.

Only it wasn't nothing, not for the rest of them.

He tried to remember what his dad had said to him that day, or even the last time they'd had a good laugh together. But it had been wiped clean. Where his dad had once been, now there was a shadow.

'So, Johnny, let's think about your death.'

Johnny opened his eyes. Mrs Cray was standing at the end of the table.

'Why do I die?' Johnny asked.

'Grief, love, despair.'

'That's not a good reason,' Johnny said.

Mrs Cray shrugged. 'People don't need reasons to die.' She paused. 'But sometimes they need reasons to live.'

'That's stupid,' he said. 'Living's just what you do. Breathe in, breathe out. You don't think about it.'

She shook her head. 'Come on, let's get this scene in the can. It's the one where you do the grand leap.'

Johnny jumped down from the table. 'At last,' he said. 'I thought we'd never get to it.'

'You sound confident.'

'Not really,' he said. But she had been right. Ever since the swim in the lake, something had changed.

Together they worked out the scene, which was mostly Johnny writhing on the table. Then, after he had practised it a few times, Mrs Cray declared it to be good enough and called everyone to the centre of the gym.

'Costumes!' she said.

She took T-shirts from a large shopping bag and handed them around. White for the swans, black for Liam and gold for the royals and courtiers.

'No wings?' Jonas said, pulling the T-shirt over his head.

It was the question Johnny had wanted to ask. But he was a prince, not a swan. He was never going to get wings.

'I decided against it,' said Mrs Cray, handing gold T-shirts and crowns to Johnny and Phoebe. 'I thought wings might look tacky. You'll show that you're swans through your dance.'

Phoebe put her crown on.

'Go on,' she said to Johnny.

195

He looked over at Liam, still worried that he would be laughed at, but Liam wasn't looking his way.

He put the crown on his head.

It felt good.

Phoebe took his arm. 'I like this,' she said. 'Shall we wear them for the rest of the day?'

Mrs Cray came up behind them as they practised walking regally.

'Fantastic! Johnny, you're suddenly really believable. But I'm sorry, I need those back. I'll give them to you on Friday for the dress rehearsal, but I can't risk them getting lost.'

Phoebe held her crown to her chest. 'But I think they suit us, don't you, Johnny?'

Johnny laughed. 'Absolutely.'

Mrs Cray shook her head. 'Bring them over to me in a minute.'

'Come on then, Queen, let's tour our kingdom one more time,' he said. Arm in arm, Johnny and Phoebe walked around the gym.

But it wasn't a school gymnasium any more; it was somewhere peaceful and beautiful, and he was happy.

For that moment, Johnny was entirely happy.

Chapter Fifteen

Thursday

The change in Johnny's status at school was immediate. By Thursday it was as if no one had ever whooped, or sneered, or made any comments about Johnny's hair or swans. As if he had always been popular.

Freed from the verbal assaults, Johnny changed too. He started to listen more in lessons – not too much, just enough to know the answers if asked. He even tried hard in a Maths test and got an average grade. And Johnny felt happy.

At lunch Johnny and Stefan sat wherever they wanted. Phoebe was with them, and they were joined by other kids from the year, who never called him Swan Boy to his face and who seemed to like him.

But it still didn't feel right. He felt like a fake. They didn't like him because of who he was.

They liked him because of who he wasn't: Liam Clark.

Walking to English, a few of the Popular kids caught up with him.

'Hey, Johnny, we're going up Primrose Hill later to hang out. Play a bit of football if Luke's remembered the ball. You wanna come?'

He shrugged. 'Nah, I'm busy, maybe another day,' he said, though there would never be another day as long as he was still an unpaid babysitter for Mojo.

Johnny had Mr Radley for English again, and the teacher picked on him straight away. 'So, Johnny, you had to leave the last lesson in a hurry, and you never did tell me what the horse called Boxer in *Animal Farm* represents.'

The edges of the teacher's mouth twitched and he stared straight at him. Johnny could tell that he wanted him not to know the answer.

In his head, Johnny stood up and said, '*The answer is the common man, Mr Radley. Boxer represents the common man.*'

If he didn't answer, the teacher would think he was stupid. But he had status now, and a chance to fit in. It was a part that he knew how to play – he had played it long enough in his old school – and being seen to be too clever would be as bad as being seen to be stupid. It was a risk. It could ruin the act.

Just like being the lead part in a dance show.

He pushed that thought from his mind.

For now he would give the teacher his satisfaction.

Johnny shrugged and shook his head. 'Dunno,' he said, and watched the teacher smile.

'Only two days to go!' Mrs Cray sounded anxious. 'And we've done brilliantly so far, but we've got so much still to do!'

She pointed over at some boys lolling by the wall.

'Come on, I want you two practising your steps for the bar scene.'

She scanned the room. 'Phoebe, Lola and Stefan, you can run through the party. The rest of you, practise the ball scene again, and remember: it's not just a question of getting your steps right. You have to stand tall, watch your hands and your expressions! Some of you look like you're being tortured!'

Mrs Cray brushed her hands through her hair. 'Right. Johnny and Liam, come over here.'

They sloped up, looking at each other warily.

'It's very last minute, but I've decided to add a scene. You've both been getting on so well that I think you can handle it. It's complicated, and we only have two days, so you'll have to get together to practise every minute you can. Break-times, after school, before school, whenever you're not asleep or in lessons. OK?'

Johnny saw his own look of horror mirrored in Liam's face.

'I'm busy,' said Liam.

'Me too,' said Johnny.

'Tough,' said Mrs Cray. 'It's just two days. Whatever it is can wait.'

Johnny shuffled his feet.

'I can't. I have to look after my little brother after school.'

'Then practise somewhere you can take him with you.'

'I can't either,' said Liam. 'I have detention after school every day this week.'

Mrs Cray smiled. 'I can get you off that.'

Johnny and Liam glared at each other again. The woman was unstoppable.

'Good. So, this scene comes directly after the drunken party. Johnny, you stumble along to the park, where you see the swans on the lake and you're overcome with their beauty, and in particular with the Black Swan, Liam.'

'No way!' said Johnny.

'Yeah,' said Liam. 'I'm not taking part in anything like that.'

'No, you don't understand,' said Mrs Cray. 'It's not love. It's more like . . . awe. Johnny, when you see the beautiful swan, it's as if a light bulb goes on in your head, and you finally know what, or who, you want to be. You don't want to be a prince, pampered and spoilt, but ultimately held prisoner by your status. You want to be wild and free. You want to swim and to fly.'

The words entered the usual way, through his ears, but to Johnny it felt as if they bypassed his brain and went directly to his heart.

To be wild.

To be free.

To swim

and to

fly?

Mrs Cray looked from one to the other.

'So, are you ready? Liam, you'll lead. You'll teach Johnny how to be a swan.'

Both boys nodded, but Johnny felt sick. He didn't want to be in the same room as Liam, let alone dance with him. Ideally he wanted to forget that Liam existed.

'Oh, and don't worry about the time. I've arranged for you two to skip the rest of your lessons, so that we can work on it all afternoon,' said Mrs Cray.

She turned on the music and Johnny recognised it instantly from the 'audition'.

Violins and a harp, in a combination so sad that it gripped him and held him to the spot.

While Johnny was transfixed by the music, Mrs Cray led Liam to the centre of the gym, and she began bending his body so that it looked like he was moving in water.

Then she twisted him and showed him how to jump over and over in a sort of hands-free cartwheel, as if he were dipping and diving through the lake.

'Now the finishing touch,' she said. Reaching Liam's arms forward, his hands met like a beak and the transformation was complete.

Until now Johnny had thought that the dancers looked like kids doing steps, more or less as Mrs Cray had shown them, but something had happened to Liam as he knelt and swayed then kicked through the water.

Johnny believed in his dance.

'Bravo!' Mrs Cray said. 'But don't forget to breathe!'

Liam froze, then dropped his arms and became himself again. 'We know!' he shouted. 'You don't have to keep saying this stuff.'

Mrs Cray looked serious. 'I repeat myself, Liam, because you have to have my voice in your head on the day. So stop arguing and drop those shoulders!'

A clarinet joined in with the strings.

'And now for your entrance, Johnny. First, just reach out towards him, but don't touch.'

Johnny felt awkward, but did as she said.

'Now follow him, but don't try to do what he does.'

Johnny ran behind Liam as he repeated his leaps and turns. He didn't need to pretend to be in awe. He was.

'Johnny, now, finally, you join in. Stand here, close to Liam, and copy what he does.'

Like a mirror had been placed between them, Johnny imitated Liam's moves exactly – the twists and turns, the way his body curled and flowed, how his arms and hands created the swan's body – and he felt like they were one person.

Mrs Cray was beaming, her hands clasped together.

'And now, Johnny, you have to stop and stand at the front of the stage looking out to the audience.'

'Why?' Johnny asked. It didn't make sense to stop.

'Because you're a human. You feel unsure of yourself. Should you really be doing this?'

Johnny shrugged. She was right.

'And now, Liam, you tempt him back. Come up behind him and put your wing around his neck to pull him back into the dance.'

Johnny panicked.

The last time Liam had put his arm around his neck, Johnny had thought he was going to die.

'Wonderful! Now tilt forward, Johnny. Liam, you go with him.'

Johnny was sweating, and his mouth was dry. This was his worst nightmare, but Mrs Cray didn't seem to notice.

'Now, Johnny, I want you to drop backwards. Liam, you are to catch Johnny and then lift him off the ground.'

Johnny felt Liam's breath behind him.

'Come on, Johnny, he won't drop you. Will you, Liam?'

'No,' said Liam.

Johnny couldn't move. Dancing with him was one thing. But trusting him was out of the question.

'Come on, Johnny,' said Mrs Cray. 'Just relax and let yourself go!'

Johnny had no choice. He shut his eyes and leant backwards. And then he felt Liam catch him, and his feet lifted from the ground.

'Perfect! And now, side by side, legs up into an arabesque and spin!'

They moved their outstretched arms slowly, like wings.

'And now, Johnny, come behind Liam.'

Johnny did as she asked.

'I want you to climb on to his back.'

'On my back?'

'Yes, Liam. He's not very heavy. And you, Liam, will raise your arms out in front to create a neck and face, and together you will become a swan.'

Johnny didn't move. No way was he climbing on to Liam Clark's back like some amorous animal on a wildlife show.

'It's too weird,' Johnny said. 'I'm not doing it.'

'But, Johnny, it'll look fantastic.'

'No, everyone will laugh.'

Mrs Cray frowned. 'Please, just give it a go.'

He shook his head.

Johnny finally had a chance to fit in at school, and he couldn't blow it. No matter how great Mrs Cray thought it would look, Johnny knew that everyone would twist it and make it into something disgusting, and he would be a laughing stock again.

He couldn't do it.

Any of it.

It was all too much.

'No,' he said. 'I'm not doing it. In fact, I'm quitting. I'm sorry, you'll have to find a new Prince.'

Johnny walked out of the gym, leaving the door swinging behind him.

Chapter Sixteen

Friday

After storming out like that, there was no way that Johnny could carry on with the show. So the next morning he faked a sore throat, and, because of how croaky his voice had been, he was allowed to stay home.

Normally, he loved a lazy day in front of the television. But Johnny was restless. He tried to forget *Swan Lake*, but twice he caught himself humming the music, and once he accidentally danced from the sofa to the bathroom.

Lunchtime was the worst. It was impossible not to think about the dress rehearsal he was missing for the show that he was never going to do.

He turned up the volume on the TV, but it didn't drown out his thoughts as he imagined someone else taking his role and attempting his leap while he was stuck at home.

But it was done. Mrs Cray had asked too much of him. She hadn't left him any choice. Had she?

At three o'clock Johnny reluctantly left the sofa and went to pick up his brother from school.

Mojo didn't hug him when he came out and wouldn't answer when Johnny asked what was wrong.

But when they got to the street Mojo said, 'Can we dance back?'

It was the last thing Johnny needed to be reminded of. And anyway, some Year Elevens from his school were coming down the road, arms round each other's shoulders and energy drinks in their hands.

He looked down at the little boy.

'No, Mojo, you're not a baby.'

'But you liked it the other day. And it was your idea.'

'Yeah, well, things have changed. I've grown up. We all have to sometime.'

Mojo squeezed his hand.

'Yeah, and that's another thing.' Johnny stopped walking. 'Maybe we should stop the hand-holding.'

Mojo let go but left his hand flapping in the air like a little bird, and Johnny had to resist the impulse to grab it back again.

'Come on, just walk next to me.'

'Can't we pretend that we're elephants and I'll hold on to your jumper like it's a tail instead?'

'No. Just walk, Mojo. Like a human.'

Mojo's mouth drooped.

'Can we go to the park? I want to play in the sandpit.'

Johnny thought about the kids from his class hanging around the park.

'No. I'm not taking you there any more either. I'm a teenager now. I can't do stuff like that.'

Mojo started crying.

'Never again?' he whispered, so quietly that Johnny could barely hear him.

He shrugged. 'Look, things need to change. I'm sorry, but you'll understand when you're my age.'

★   ★   ★

Back at the flat their mum was pink-cheeked and the smell of baking and cleaning products filled the air.

Mojo raised his nose and sniffed. 'Is dinner ready? Crying has made me hungry.'

'You've been crying again? Poor love,' she said, helping him with his jacket. 'But I'm sorry dinner is going to be a while because I'm making something extra special.'

'But I'm hungry,' Mojo moaned.

'Well, you can have a snack but we're going to have to wait for dinner because I've got some friends coming over this evening.'

Mojo frowned. 'So that stuff that smells nice isn't for me?'

'It's for all of us. But we'll be having it later with my friends.'

'Which friends?' he asked.

'Belinda and Jane.'

'Who's Belinda and Jane?'

'Mum's new friends,' said Johnny. 'She's moving on.'

She shot him an angry look. 'It's not like that.'

'Why?' Mojo said. 'You don't need new friends. You've got old friends at the old house. Anyway, you don't need friends cos you're a mum.'

Her voice was tight. 'Even mums need friends, Mojo. Besides I still have my old friends, but they're a bit far away now, so it's OK to get new ones too.'

Mojo pursed his lips and trembled. 'Why does everything have to keep changing? Johnny told me that we can't even hold hands any more or dance or anything!' Tears were running down his cheeks and there was a wet trail coming from his nose. 'But I like holding hands and dancing! And I like things how they used to be!' He flared his nostrils and hunched his shoulders up to his ears, and shouted, 'And I'm never going to get on to the sunny side of the board!'

Mojo ran into the kitchen and slammed the door behind him.

'What was all that about? Why would you say that you can't hold hands or dance any more?'

Johnny shrugged. 'He was being really babyish and I just told him to grow up a bit.'

She frowned. 'But he is a baby.'

'No, he's not, he's five.'

'Where's this coming from, Johnny? You're usually so nice with him.'

'I'm still nice with him.'

'And why's he talking about the sunny side of the board? If he's been in trouble again the school should've told me.'

She looked up and sniffed.

'Oh no, I forgot about the pie!'

She ran out of the room.

There was silence, then:

'OH MY GOD!' In the kitchen Johnny's mum was staring straight ahead, her mouth sagging, like she'd had a stroke.

Johnny grabbed her. 'Mum, are you OK? What's the matter? Is it the pie?'

She tried to speak but, instead of words, a strange sound that was mostly air came out.

'Mum? Shall I call an ambulance?' he said, clutching her arms.

She still stared ahead.

'Mum? Mum, talk to me! What's happened?'

She shook her head gently, and a tear pooled and spilled out on to her cheek.

Then he realised what she was staring at.

The cloth was on the floor. The table was revealed.

'Oh. Mojo's drawings,' he said. 'I'm sorry, I really am. Please don't be angry. I'm sure they'll come off with a bit of scrubbing. It's my fault really cos I didn't get him any paper from school, like I promised.'

She carried on staring at the table with the same expression of shock that she had worn the day his dad had died.

'St Raymond,' she breathed.

'What? Look, I'll clean it off so you can sort out the dinner.'

He opened the under-sink cupboard and got out the cleaner and a sponge. She still didn't move, so he started spraying the table. Straight away the pictures began to blur and bleed, and the foam turned multicoloured.

His mum's eyes were still blank, like she was in a trance, and Johnny was just thinking that she was going a bit over the top when something caught his eye.

'Patron saint of secrets,' she whispered.

Then he started to follow the spiral of the drawings.

In the beginning there were lots of superhero adventures, mostly Mojo's cats fighting dragons that looked like vomiting green horses with scales and tales, and Johnny's feather, glistening.

Then, gradually, the drawings changed.

By the time he was looking at the third ring in, Mojo was drawing people. Real people. Johnny, himself, his friends, their mum and dad.

There were words too, in bubbles, like the comics Johnny had given him, so he could tell that they were seeing his memories: his first day at school, a Christmas tree surrounded by presents, next door's dog getting run over, the World Cup, their dad drinking beer with his friends, Mum making a birthday cake.

In between, little cats and dragons were hidden in the everyday scenes, peeking out round doorways or visible flying past windows.

And then the central rings, tiny and detailed, packed together so tightly that Johnny could hardly see them – drawings that Mojo must have finished in secret.

His dad and Mojo at the dinner table.

His dad telling Mojo, '*Eet yor broccoli.*'

Mojo crying and saying, '*It's yuk!*'

And the final speech bubble.

Mojo shouting, '*I hate you, Dady! I wish you wud die.*'

His dad's face, a tear on his cheek.

And in the very centre, in deep red ink,

their dad's heart

cracked in two.

Johnny stood with the cleaning stuff still in his hands, unable to move, looking at the picture of his dad. Then he squirted more cleaner on it and he kept squirting and squirting, until the centre of the table was a cone of white foam covering his dad's heart like an acrid snow scene.

His mum seemed to wake up then because she came up behind him and took the sponge and the cleaner.

'It's OK,' she said, sobbing. 'It's OK.'

'Mojo didn't do it, did he?' Johnny was shouting. 'You can't kill someone with words, can you?'

She put her arm round him, her face wet with tears. 'No, of course not. He didn't kill him. Your dad had a dodgy heart.' She held him tight. 'I can't believe Mojo never told anyone. He kept it a secret for all these months. I feel so bad.'

'You need to tell him it's not true.'

His mum dried her eyes. 'I will. I'll talk to him now.'

Johnny heard her calling Mojo's name, and he stared at the melting image of his dad's heart as he wiped the tears from his own eyes.

'Johnny!' She ran back into the kitchen. 'Johnny, he's gone!'

'What?'

'The front door's open and he's taken his shoes!'

Johnny jumped up and ran out to the hallway.

'You stay here in case he comes back,' he told his mum, then pulled on his trainers and ran down the stairs two at a time.

Outside, he shielded his eyes from the sun and looked up and down.

There was no sign of Mojo.

Where could he be? He only knew the way to school and the park. And maybe the Tube.

Would he try and go home? Back to Tooting?

Johnny ran all the way down the street, scanning from left to right as he went.

'Have you seen a little boy, black hair, coming this way?' he asked everyone he saw.

Heads shook, answers drowned out by the noise from the road.

He reached the Tube station. 'Have you seen a little boy, black hair, this big?' he asked the flower seller, bringing his hand up to his waist to show Mojo's height.

'No, sorry.'

'I have,' the *Big Issue* seller sitting opposite called out.

'Yes? Where?'

'Other side of the road. He came up here, then turned and went back the other way. I thought his mum must be back there. Run away, has he?'

Johnny didn't wait to reply. He headed back towards the flat, then ran straight past it.

It was possible that Mojo had gone home to face his mum. But, somehow, Johnny doubted it.

He ran as fast as he could, but he had never felt so slow and useless. The green man changed to red as he reached the crossing at the start of Primrose Hill. Lorries thundered past, blowing up the dust. He imagined Mojo trying to cross the road and he shuddered.

At the park he ran to the top of the hill. People were playing, kite-flying, walking dogs, filming something.

'I've lost my little brother!' he said to anyone who would listen. 'He's small, only five, he's got black hair.'

People looked concerned but shook their heads.

Johnny ran down the hill. Near the bottom he saw a group of boys with trendy haircuts and maroon jumpers: the Populars.

'Hey, Johnny!' someone called over. 'What you doing?'

'I've lost my little brother. I think he might be around here.'

'What does he look like?'

'Like me. But smaller,' he said. 'And he might be acting a bit weird. Like an animal or something.' He didn't care what they thought now.

'We'll let you know if we see him,' they said.

But Johnny was gone, heading down the hill towards the play area.

Inside he was screaming:

PLEASE BE THERE. PLEASE BE THERE. PLEASE BE THERE. PLEASE BE THERE. PLEASE BE THERE. PLEASE BE THERE. PLEASE BE THERE. PLEASE BE THERE. PLEASE BE THERE. PLEASE BE THERE. I'LL DO ANYTHING IF HE'S THERE!

Johnny spotted him before he even got inside the play area.

Mojo was sitting in the sandpit by himself.

It looked like there had been some sort of struggle; the other children were keeping out of his way or standing crying with their adults.

'Mojo!' Johnny called.

Mojo looked up at him.

Lines running down his cheeks from his eyes sparkled with sand in the sunshine.

'I'm sorry,' Mojo said and he raised his arms.

Johnny picked him up and held him tight.

'Don't ever run off again.'

'I'm not sorry about that. I got here all by myself. I am old enough now. I've grown up.' He sniffed and looked down. 'I'm sorry about Dad.'

Johnny squeezed him tighter. 'I know you are. But you don't need to say sorry because it wasn't your fault he died, Mojo. You didn't do it.'

He put him back on the sand and sat down next to him.

'I did.'

'No, it was heart disease. It wasn't you.' He put his arm around Mojo's shoulder.

Mojo was silent for a moment. 'Where did you think I'd gone?'

'I dunno. I thought maybe back to Tooting on the Tube.'

Mojo smiled. 'Don't you mean dragon?'

Johnny laughed. 'Obviously. Anyway, no more secrets.'

'OK.' He frowned. 'Apart from the secret about you going out at night and leaving me.'

'Yeah, that one's OK,' Johnny said.

'And the one about the letter and the glass thing I threw?'

'Maybe we should tell Mum about that.'

'Really?'

'Yeah. I think she'll understand now. Come on, we need to get back.'

Johnny stood up and held his hand out, but Mojo didn't take it.

'Don't take me home yet,' Mojo said. 'I don't want to see Mum.'

'We have to go. She's worried. You just went without telling us. You could've been run over.'

'But I wasn't.' He smiled and some of the sand on his face flaked off.

'Yeah, about what I said about being more grown up – I definitely didn't mean for you to go wandering around by yourself.'

Johnny reached down and took Mojo's hand. 'I think we should stick to the old ways for a bit longer. Maybe until you're seven. Or eight. Come on.'

Mojo widened his big eyes. 'But can we go and see the ducks first? Please?'

Johnny sighed. 'OK, just for a minute.'

He was worried about their mum, but he took Mojo across the road and on to the bridge that led to Regent's Park.

As they leant over and looked into the water, a swan passed underneath and Johnny smiled.

'Do you know they can break a person's arm?' he told him.

But Mojo wasn't listening. He was already tugging Johnny away.

They followed the path, where the thick reeds blocked their view, then carried on until they arrived at the open space where the scummy water licked the grass and the ducks and swans and geese gathered to beg tourists for bread.

But Mojo kept on pulling him. He had seen something in the distance and he was running now, right to the end of the lake.

The music came to them on a breeze.

Violins.

Oboes.

Harps.

Clarinets.

Then Johnny saw them in the distance: ten men and women, maybe more, standing in a row with someone in front talking to them.

'Come on, it's a show!' said Mojo, his tears forgotten.

The pair ran together, still holding hands. Johnny didn't care that the other kids from school were somewhere nearby and that he might ruin the reputation he had only just won.

He didn't want it anyway.

But, as they got closer, Johnny could see that it wasn't a show. The people weren't in costumes, just jogging bottoms and T-shirts.

They were strong and fit. Poised and ready, stretching their bodies or gently jogging on the spot, waiting for a cue.

'What does that say?' Mojo pointed to the sign placed in front of them. Johnny read it aloud.

Rehearsal. Please do not disturb.
The Management, Regent's Park Open Air Theatre.

'What does it mean?'

'They're practising for a show in the theatre over there.'

'A dance show?'

'Yes. I think so.'

'They're dancers, like you!' Mojo said, and he smiled.

Johnny laughed. 'Not really like me.'

'I want to watch,' said Mojo.

So they sat on the grass and waited. Then a flock of swans glided over and stopped close to the dancers as well. It looked like they were waiting too.

Finally the woman in front changed the music and the dancers sprung into action, rehearsing a scene, doing steps and leaps and turns that Johnny would never have thought possible.

'How do they even do that?' Mojo asked.

Johnny shrugged. 'Training, I guess. And talent. I mean, it would take more than . . .'

The principal dancer left the group and peeled off his damp T-shirt. As the low evening light bounced off the lake and hit him, it highlighted the silver sheen of his chest.

Johnny took a breath, and put his hand to his own chest.

Mojo was still watching the dancers, his head on one side.

'Johnny, d'you know what?' he said. 'They *are* like you.'

Johnny only just managed to speak. 'What d'you mean?'

He shrugged. 'Well, they're really good at dancing too.'

There was a gentle splash as one of the swans climbed out of the water. It waddled over and sat down within touching distance of them.

'Johnny!'

The group of Populars had spotted him. They came running over and the swan stood up, looking disgusted, and waddled back into the water.

'You found him!' one said.

'Yeah. He was in the sandpit.'

'So, d'you wanna come and play some footie?'

Johnny looked over at the dancers and then at Mojo.

'No thanks, I'd better get him home. But another day.' And he meant it. Maybe next time he would.

Johnny and Mojo climbed the stairs, still holding hands.

His mum had been waiting by the front door. She grabbed Mojo and hugged him so tight that Johnny wondered if he could breathe.

'Oh, Mojo,' she said, wiping away the tears that started flowing again. 'Please don't ever do that again. I was so worried.'

Mojo's bottom lip wobbled.

'Come on inside,' she said, and sat him down on the sofa with a cup of hot chocolate.

She knelt down next to him.

'We, er, we saw the table,' she said, stroking his hand.

Mojo dipped his head.

His mum put her hand gently underneath his chin and raised his face again.

'Mojo, do you remember the time when we'd been to a wedding in Brighton, and you were playing in the waves and you got knocked off your feet? Your dad was in his best suit and he went in to get you.'

Mojo nodded. 'Yes, it was horrible.'

'Well, shall I tell you a secret?'

He nodded again.

'Your dad couldn't swim.'

Mojo frowned.

'He'd never learnt. But the moment he realised that you were in danger, he didn't think about himself because he loved you. And what about the time when we went to that posh French restaurant with Auntie Rose?'

Mojo giggled. 'We were naughty.'

His mum smiled back. 'Yes, your dad kept making the frogs' legs dance the cancan, and then the two of you got the giggles and I had to send you both outside until you calmed down.'

Mojo laughed at the memory.

'And,' she said, softening her voice, 'do you know that I only saw your dad cry twice?'

Mojo shook his head.

'Once when Johnny was born, and once when you were born. And it wasn't because you were hideously ugly. He cried because you made him so happy. And every single day after that you made him happy. Happier than anything else in the world.'

'But I said something terrible to him,' Mojo mumbled.

'I know. But he knew you didn't mean it, and that wasn't what damaged his heart. Sometimes people die, and it's not fair.' She paused. 'But we can't bring them back, so the only thing we can do is to remember them and be happy that they lived.'

'I'll eat broccoli now,' said Mojo.

'You don't have to,' said his mum.

'And what about the table? Aren't you angry about that?'

'No. I'm not angry. I had to wash your pictures off because they got smudged,' she said. 'But, you know, I thought they were wonderful. Anyway, it's all white again now, so you can do new drawings – your super-heroes, strange creatures, even us or Dad. Whatever you want.'

'Can I? I'm allowed?' He turned to Johnny. 'See? You were wrong! Mum says I *can* draw on the table!'

Johnny smiled. 'Yeah, who knew, eh, Mojo?'

'So, Mojo, from now on, if there's something bothering you, you need to tell me.'

Mojo frowned. 'Well . . . it's not bothering me really, but there is a letter from my teacher that Johnny says I have to show you.'

She nodded. 'OK, maybe I'll look at that tomorrow. The main thing is no more secrets.' She turned to Johnny. 'That applies to you too.'

'Me?' Johnny was surprised. He had thought this was about Mojo.

'Yes. I know things have been difficult since we moved. And I also know you think I rely on you too much.'

Johnny shrugged. 'No, not really.'

'Well, maybe you're too nice to say so, but I think you're right. And now that I've been there a few months, I've asked if I can change my hours at work so that I can pick up Mojo more. So you can join a club, start to mix a bit, make some new friends.'

Johnny nodded. 'That would be good.'

She put her arm around his shoulders.

'I also know something's been going on at school. Is it that boy, Stefan?'

Johnny laughed. 'Stefan? No, Mum, I told you, he's great. I'll bring him round soon so you can meet him properly. And everything's fine at school. I mean, there *was* something, but I think it's sorted now.'

He took a breath. 'It's, like, when you join a new

school and people don't know who you are, you start to forget who you are too.'

She put her hand on his knee. 'You've just got to be yourself, Johnny.'

'Yeah, you could've told me that two months ago!'

Just then Mojo sniffed. 'What is that nasty smell?'

'Oh, that was the dinner I was making,' his mum said. 'It's ruined now.'

Mojo wailed, 'Well, what are we going to eat then? I'm starved! Those kids at the playground wouldn't give me any of their seaweed!'

Just then the doorbell rang.

'Ah, the backup plan has arrived,' his mum said.

Johnny answered the door. Two women, about his mum's age, were standing there holding bulging plastic bags. The familiar aroma coming from them made his mouth water.

'Hi,' the blonde one said. 'I'm Belinda and this is Jane. You must be Johnny.'

'Kebabs?' he said. 'Come on in.'

Chapter Seventeen

Saturday

Although it was only eleven o'clock in the morning, Mrs Cray was standing by the hall door wearing an evening dress, big loop earrings and full make-up. But wrinkles were set deep into her brow.

The tickets had been sold, and the first few families were already sitting in their hard plastic seats, but neither the Prince nor the Black Swan were there, and both had been missing for the dress rehearsal.

When Johnny had said he was quitting, she hadn't taken it seriously. But maybe he had really meant it.

The head teacher, the school nurse and the new woman from the art department were already sitting in the front row.

She knew that it was the talk of the staffroom, and though no one had said it to her face, it was obvious that they all thought it was a ridiculous idea. Even she had to admit that perhaps she had been wrong, that her plan to turn around the more challenging students via dance had been unrealistic.

She shook her head. They had been so promising.

Liam was a natural dancer. His body was small and lean, but he was strong and so graceful.

And Johnny . . . well, he had that fire burning inside him, the thing that makes a dancer into an artist. She had thought he had what it took; she had been so sure.

She looked at the clock on the wall.

Fifteen minutes until the curtain rose – on what? An empty stage? A few lost swans and an evil magician?

She rolled her shoulders and wriggled her jaw to relieve the tension. Maybe it was time to give up teaching. If she had misjudged this so badly, was she really up to it any more? Maybe she could work part-time at the technical college, teach older students, or adults even.

Teenagers were just too unpredictable.

Out of the corner of her eye she saw someone walk past the window. Liam.

Mrs Cray unlocked the glazed door and went on to the playing fields.

'Liam, there you are! I thought you weren't coming.'

Liam shrugged. 'I wasn't.'

'But you did.'

He looked past her. 'Yeah, well, I thought I might as well get it over with.'

Mrs Cray smiled. 'I'm glad. Well, get changed and I'll see you in there.' She paused by the door. 'I meant what I said, Liam. You're not going to look stupid. You'll look magnificent. Now go in and get ready. I've left your costume on the bench.'

Liam snorted, but she thought that she could detect a faint smile underneath it.

Mrs Cray nearly ran into Johnny as she went back inside.

'Ah, so the star arrives at last.' She folded her arms. 'Where were you yesterday?'

Johnny hung his head. 'I'm sorry. I was sick. But I'm here now. Did you . . . Can I still have my part?'

She wasn't going to let him off that easily.

'You've barely practised that scene with Liam. I just don't know how this is going to go.'

'I know I've let you down,' he said. 'But I think it will be OK.'

She raised her eyebrows.

'It will be better than ever, miss. I promise. Cos I know what you mean now. I really do – I just needed some time to work it out for myself.'

Mrs Cray took a deep breath. Then her toothy grin broke through, and she hugged him with her cage-fighter arms.

'Of course you can still have your part. I'm so glad you're here, Johnny. Go and get changed – your costume's waiting. We're on in ten minutes.'

Backstage, Stefan was sitting on a bench looking sick, and Phoebe was massaging his shoulders.

'All right?' Johnny said.

He nodded. 'Nerves. I thought I'd be fine, but I've been on the toilet all morning.'

Phoebe gave him a final squeeze and said, 'There you go.' She patted him on the back and went to the mirror to do her hair.

Johnny raised his eyebrows.

'Something going on with you two that I should know about?'

'Course not. We're just good friends. I mean, I think she'd probably like more, but I'm really busy with school and work and stuff, so . . .'

Johnny laughed. 'Yeah, I believe you. Thousands wouldn't.'

Then he went into the cupboard that was doubling as a dressing room and put on the costume: white shorts, gold T-shirt and a crown that he fixed in place with hairgrips.

He looked at himself in the mirror that was propped up in the corner, and he smiled.

He didn't look like a prince. The T-shirt was too big, and the crown looked naff. But what did he expect for a school show?

He pushed open the door.

'What d'you think?'

Stefan and Phoebe bowed.

'Your Royal Highness the Swan Boy,' Phoebe said. 'You don't look too shabby.'

'I'm gonna go and see if my dad's here,' said Stefan.

They followed him into the wings of the stage.

Stefan groaned.

'What is it?' asked Johnny.

'He's brought my sister!'

'What's wrong with your sister?' said Phoebe.

'She's twice the size and ten times as tough as me, but without my winning personality,' he said.

They peered round the curtain. Johnny spotted her straight away, sitting with Stefan's dad.

'She looks just like you in make-up,' said Johnny, laughing.

'We only have one face in our family,' said Stefan. 'Unfortunately.'

And then Johnny saw his mum and brother arrive.

Mojo was chatting and smiling. Like the old Mojo. Johnny had missed him.

Coming up behind them were Belinda and Jane. The kebabs they'd brought round the night before had been the best that Johnny had ever tasted. It had been a good evening. Belinda and Jane were thoughtful and funny, and they had made a fuss of Mojo. When they heard about the show they had begged to be allowed to come too, and, though he hardly knew them, Johnny was glad that they were there.

'Where's Clark?' Stefan said.

Johnny went to find him.

Liam was outside again, in his black costume, chewing gum and staring across the field.

Johnny pushed open the door and sat down.

Liam looked at him and sneered. 'Does that thing follow you around?'

A swan was sitting at the far end of the playing field.

Johnny shrugged. 'No.' Then he thought about it. 'Actually, I dunno. Maybe.'

Liam turned to look at him then. 'You look like an idiot.'

'I know. So do you.'

Liam laughed.

'We didn't practise,' Johnny said.

'Nah.'

Liam blew out a large pink bubble, then sucked it back into his mouth.

'I wasn't going to do it,' Johnny said.

'Me neither.'

'Our dance is a bit, y'know ...' He raised his eyebrows.

Liam laughed. 'Yeah, I know. But then I realised that they'd probably make me do the litter pick if I didn't turn up.' He did jazz hands. 'So here I am.'

They sat in silence for a moment, then Johnny said, 'Liam, are we all right now?'

Liam blew a last bubble, then spat the gum out on to the field, too pink among the blades of grass.

'I don't know what you're talking about,' he said, and he went back inside.

Johnny held back for a minute, trying to empty his mind, and then Stefan stuck his head round the door.

'Why are you out here? Get a move on. We're about to start, and we can't do it without the star.'

Back inside, the swans were warming up.

'One two–three, one two–three.' Jonas was counting the beat.

They were all dressed in white with a black point painted down their foreheads like a beak.

Johnny smiled. They looked nothing like swans, but they looked good.

Mrs Cray ran in.

'Two minutes!'

Two minutes?

It felt too soon for Johnny. He began to stretch his muscles and tried to focus. But it was hard. His head was still full of Mojo and the table, and Liam, and the big question.

Would he do it?

He brushed his fingers through the white streak, then put his hand under his T-shirt and felt his chest. Hard with muscles now, yet soft and silky warm with the feathers, just like the dancer in the park.

Mrs Cray appeared again. 'One minute!' she said. 'Remember: shoulders down, long necks and breathe!'

Johnny went to the wings as the lights dimmed.

Mrs Cray came up behind him and put her hand on his arm.

'Are you ready, Johnny?'

'I think so. I mean, I hope so.'

'Well, I can tell you this,' she said. 'I would hardly recognise you as the boy I met a few weeks ago. But it's up to you in the end. You're the Prince and it's your story.'

Johnny knew what she meant then.

She was giving him permission.

To be himself.

To be brave.

To be honest.

To do it his way. Through the darkness of the audience he saw Mojo's pale face and big eyes.

And then it was time to begin.

Scene one was difficult at first. The energy running through him like a current made his muscles stiff, and his brain was dulled by the adrenaline.

Then the music changed and suddenly he was caught up in it, his body remembering all the steps so that his mind could forget them and focus on the feelings.

And Just Be.

There was no time to worry about the scene with Liam before they were there onstage, enemies dancing together, working as one to create something bigger. And when they reached the end and he climbed on to Liam's back, and the audience clapped and shouted, Johnny knew that Mrs Cray had been right.

And then all that was left was the final scene, where he would dance with the swans, and then climb on to the bed and die.

Johnny stood in the wings, waiting for his cue.

The table was in the centre of the stage as a bed, and a spotlight shone down on it.

Mrs Cray stood next to him, her hand on his shoulder.

'You've done well so far,' she said. 'I'm proud of you. Now go and do what you've got to do. You've stuck to my script, but now it's your story.'

His story.

Johnny nodded.

The music rose and his heartbeat merged with the sound as his muscles twitched, and he could feel every hair, every tufty feather, stand on end.

On cue he walked slowly to the back of the stage.

The swans came in and danced with and around him.

And then he climbed on to the bed.

He wasn't supposed to be up there yet, so the other dancers looked confused, and it took a while for the spotlight to find him.

But when it finally encircled him, like the moon on the lake, Johnny wasn't afraid to be in it.

With Mrs Cray's voice in his head, he relaxed his shoulders, lengthened his neck and took a deep breath.

He pulled the hairgrips from the crown and tossed it away, then he peeled off the gold T-shirt and dropped it to the ground.

Then, with his arms crossed over his chest, Johnny began to spin.

And as he turned faster and faster, the force pulled back his shoulders until he couldn't resist any longer.

He had to let them unfurl into wings.

His wings.

And then he jumped from the bed.

He ran towards the front of the stage.

And he flew.

Acknowledgements

Big thanks to my superstar agent, Julia Churchill, who always has faith in my unusual ideas; my genius editor Sarah Odedina; and amazing Madeleine Stevens for taking on *Swan Boy* and helping to make it SO much better; not forgetting Nathan Burton for the cover, which I absolutely ❤; and Claire Whitston, who was there at the beginning. I've been so lucky!

Thanks are also due to my husband Dylan for pretty much everything, and my children: Morgan, who continues to inspire me; Eddie, whose generosity of spirit extends to reading really bad first drafts; and Harvey, who is hard to please, so a good barometer for how interesting a story is.

I'm so grateful to my dog-walking friends who let me moan, the Team ITS for the love and laughs, Sarah Crossan for the friendship and koalas, and to all my other brilliant writing friends who helped and encouraged me with this book: Lisa Heathfield, Tatum Flynn, Pip Jones, Allan Boroughs, Allie Rogers, Suzanna Drew-Edwards, Lucy Cage, Deborah Price and Sandi Fikuart.

But most of all, thanks to my mum and dad, my sister and brother, and to the coal bunker in the garden from which I learnt to fly.

www.rocktheboat.london